WHISPERING RIDGE

dianesoldwestnovels.com

Other Books by Diane M. Cece

The Trails Southwest Trilogy

Book 1: Trails Southwest

Book 2: The Cattle Drive from Southwest

Book 3: The Rodeo Southwest

WHISPERING RIDGE

Book 4 in the Southwest Series

Best wishes to my friends Bob + Linda.

As ever,

Diane

Diane M. Cece

Rev. date: 08/19/2014

To order additional copies of this book, contact:
Xlibris LLC
1-888-795-4274
www.Xlibris.com
Orders@Xlibris.com
636601

CONTENTS

For Mom and Dad

My heart beats because of you.
Your spiritual love for each other during seventy-three-and-a-half years
of marriage has held my life together.

Thank you for always being there for me. God bless.

Acknowledgments

The author would like to take this opportunity to thank several individuals without whose assistance this series would not have been possible.

Thank you, Mary Flores, publishing consultant; Michael Green, submissions representative; Lorie Adams, author services representative; Heidi White, Monica Williams, David Castro, Ronald Flor, Jane Javier, marketing services; Clifford Young, author services; Tony Hermano, author consultant; Lloyd Griffith, James Colonia, manuscript services; Lloyd Baron, web design; Amerie Evans, senior book consultant; Gerald Rae Albacite, and Chris Anthony Ferrer, copyediting, and Leo Montano, customer services.

Thank you, John Covert, for designing my website, www. DianesOldWestNovels.com. John, you have been a tremendous inspiration for getting this author technologically advanced.

Thanks again, everyone, for being a part of my life and my work. You are the best ever that anyone can have available at their right side.

CHAPTER I

THE HUNTING TRIP

It was a long time since the Nevada Kid and Smokey decided to go on a hunting trip in the mountains, and they were determined to take some time off from ranching and visit their friend Cappie, the fur trapper. Nevada's new wife, Ricki, would be good at overseeing the ranch and the cowboys

Nevada had working for him on the Flying T2 Ranch, so taking off for a week in the mountains was not a problem for the new ranch owner.

Nevada couldn't wait to get into the lush ponderosa pine forests and see the rushing streams and the mountain lake Cappie spoke of, along with the aspens mixed in with the pines in the high country of the sierras.

Jim Cappieona, nicknamed Cappie by the cowboys, was in his late thirties or early forties. He liked living in the mountains above Yuma. Cappie was raised in the mountains by a cougar, not by an old mountain lion as a popular song suggests. He had curly black hair, with cheeks that caved in on the oval-shaped face, broad shoulders, and a thin waistline, and he was a trapper by trade. He could read sign and knew the backwoods like the palm of his hand. He wore tight buckskins, which enhanced this fine figure of a man. A loner, he roamed wild and free like a black panther. No one owned him or tried to own him. Usually in the springtime, he slipped down out of the mountains to join a trail drive for kicks, sell his furs to traders, or visit folks he knew at the neighboring ranches around the areas of Yuma and Tucson, Arizona.

The Nevada Kid and Smokey became very good friends with Cappie while spending time working with him at the O'Connor Cattle Ranch in Yuma and the Broken Arrow Ranch during rodeo season, near Smithville, Arizona. The three of them became inseparable while boarding there at the bunkhouse. Cappie taught Nevada everything he knew about cutting rawhide strips for lacing and making bridles, halters, cinch straps, and flank straps for the rough-stock animals. It was a great-paying job for the Nevada Kid to have while competing in the rodeo circuit and earning money to buy the ranch he now owns.

They decided one pack horse was enough for all their gear, so Nevada and Smokey gathered everything together that they would need for the trail and the hunting trip. They were never at Cappie's cabin, but they had a good idea as to where it was from hearing Cappie tell stories about it often enough.

The Nevada Kid was twenty-eight years old, about five feet ten inches tall with broad shoulders, and those shoulders were strong and muscular. He had Cherokee Indian blood in him from his father's side of the family and Norseman or Viking blood from his mother's family lines. He had restless blue eyes that will wash over you and drink up every detail they see. His high Cherokee cheekbones, set off by a Viking nose and full curving lips, gave him a very handsome, masculine look that stood out in a crowd and made his presence noticed whenever he entered into a room. What also stood out about him was his energetic restlessness that reached into his very soul and turned into aspiring, power-hungry ambition.

Smokey, on the other hand, was about six feet tall with a relatively thick and sturdy build. His curly black hair fell softly into a ringlet on his forehead, which bounced around when he moved, and his leather-tough skin was tanned dark from the hot sun. He was about thirty-five years old and was tough-looking, except for his laugh, which had a cute gentleness that gave away his easygoing attitude. Smokey was generous and impulsive, which attracted the girls to him for his kidding, laughing ways. Although Smokey had a great deal of common sense and was intelligent, he was a bit on the carefree and lazy side.

From Yuma, they took the trail that wraps up along the face of the Gila Mountains and traveled eight miles up toward the top of the mountain. The trail was not well traveled and would be a two-day trip up the stony, rubbly mountain. It would be slow going and, in some places, a rough trail surface where mud and sand caused unsteady footing on the horse's hooves. The old route they were taking was often used by Indians, the Spanish, and gold-rush travelers. They encountered some rocks up to six inches in diameter along loose, rough trail surfaces but found them passable on horseback where a shelf on the mountain opened wide enough for them to go around the bad spots.

The climate for the month of February averaged between a low of forty-eight degrees at night and a high of seventy-five degrees during the day. Rainfall for the month usually averaged around twenty-eight inches.

When night moved in, they decided to make a dry camp and settled down to a quiet evening, making camp under a cluster of piñon pine, which grows at the lower elevations. Its cone is relatively small with woody scales, and the nuts of the pine are edible. This camp offered the horses a good rest from what was a very labored trail climb. Bacon, beans, some nuts from the tree, and a jackrabbit's misfortune for crossing Nevada's path made a good supper for them. After supper, they fashioned a smoke and sat on their bedrolls, relaxing for a bit. When his smoke was finished, Nevada decided to sing and hum the song "Wayward Wind" as he had done so many times while night herding. In answer to his melodic singing, a song dog wailed—a wild coyote, the keeper of the night and a majestic predator—alerting them to the danger for their horses and themselves. The coyote sounded like the animal was not far off from the camp or perhaps moving in close to the camp. Nevada and Smokey's eyes locked in a glance for a few seconds with each other. Nevada's singing being suddenly interrupted caused them to simultaneously check the rounds in their pistols and rifles, an automatic reaction of self-defense.

The coyote was moving in close enough to camp to necessitate using their rifles, so they lay down on their stomachs on the bedrolls with their rifles ready to shoot anything that moves or strikes. The horses were luring the animal in for a kill as it picked up their scent and circled the camp looking for fresh prey. It was slinking within fifteen yards of Nevada, and he could not see it or hear it. Smokey caught a movement to the right of Nevada, low and in the underbrush. Just then, Nevada locked gazes for two seconds with a big male coyote and froze in awe. Smokey's gun roared with a *boom*, rattling Nevada's nerves.

"Nevada, were you just gonna admire that animal or shoot it?" was Smokey's question.

"I never saw him until the second just before you shot him," replied Nevada.

"He was circling the camp. Picked up our scent and the scent of the horses. When he saw you, he froze, silently getting ready to pounce. I picked him off just in time as his back feet were moving and setting up for the leap. Coyotes like lying motionless in the grass, watching with their keen predator eyes, just waiting for the kill. You're lucky he didn't pounce on you while you were admiring him." Smokey laughed.

"Thanks, Smokey. I was lucky you saw him first. I must be slowing down."

"We will field-dress him out here and throw him on the pack horse. Cappie might like to have this fur."

They banked the fire for the night, and the rest of the evening proved to be quiet as they slept in a sound, relaxing sleep, with nothing but the whispering of the mountain ridges to serenade them into a peaceful repose.

Chapter II

CAPPIE'S MOUNTAIN HOME

In the morning, they ate a quick snack of beef jerky, cleaned up the campsite, and headed up the trail to the top of the mountain. The trail leveled out, and they followed it across the top of the mountain ridges through a dense-forested tree line of ponderosa pine and Gambel oak and past heavy underbrush. Wandering past a mountain lake and a rushing stream, they continued on following the trail, not stopping for lunch, until they came up to a clearing in the woods and a trapper's cabin partially made of logs and clapboard. This had to be the cabin Cappie described so many times in his stories at the cow camps. They tethered the horses at the rail and knocked on the cabin door. No answer. They knocked again, this time calling out to Cappie. Still no answer. They tried the door, and it was not locked, so they stealthily entered the cabin.

The mice were finishing a meal that was left half-eaten on the table. Cappie's sidearm was hanging on a wall peg, and his rifle was on pegs over the fireplace. No Cappie in sight. So where was Cappie?

"Hey, Nevada. Maybe he is out checking traplines," said Smokey.

"Without his rifle or his sidearm?" replied Nevada. "I don't think so. That's not likely."

Smokey started throwing out the stale, dry food and cleaning up the table and dishes as the mice scattered away. "He must have left in a hurry, Nevada, to leave food on the table and not clean anything up. It's just not like Cappie," said Smokey. "He would never leave anything lying around the bunkhouse. He always picked up after himself." Smokey dumped out the stale coffee, washed the pot, and put on a fresh pot of coffee.

"I know," replied Nevada. "He always wanted tabletops cleaned up when I worked with him in the tack shop at the Broken Arrow Ranch. He didn't want one scrap of leather or piece of soft grass roping left lying around. Whatever was considered to be scrap had to be put immediately into the scrap barrels."

Cappie's two pack mules were in the pole corral, and his horse was missing. So wherever he was, they figured he was riding his horse. Smokey went outside and took care of their horses, Tacco and Jawbone, and their pack horse, Lazy Daisy, unloading them and adding the animals to the pole corral with Cappie's pack horses. Smokey hung up the coyote hide on the rack made from aspen trees, which Cappie used for drying animal skins and furs, then he brought their gear inside the cabin.

"Something is not right here," said Nevada. Why would Cappie ride off on his horse and not take any self-protection with him?"

"Beats me," said Smokey. "All his pelts and furs are gone too, but the pack horses are still here. Let's make some supper, and maybe he will be back by early evening, and we can get some straight answers."

"You start supper, Smokey. I want to look around outside." Nevada went outside and looked around. Wagon tracks only a day or so old and several tracks from a group of horses. Evidently, the horses were escorting a wagon, from the way it looked. There was a possibility that Cappie had a wagon and was taking the furs and pelts to a nearby mountain town in the wagon. If, perhaps, they followed the wagon tracks, would they catch up with Cappie? Nevada went back inside the cabin.

"There are wagon tracks outside and lots of horse tracks. What do you say we follow the wagon tracks and horse tracks in the morning if Cappie does not come back tonight?" said Nevada.

"Sounds like a good plan to me," said Smokey.

They were eating dinner when they were suddenly interrupted by a bedraggled-looking man coming through the door without knocking. Nevada's gun hand drew lightning fast, beating the movement coming in through the door. The fast draw startled and frightened the stranger.

Jonah was a big, overweight fellow who ran a moonshine still as a profitable business on the mountainside. His eyes were brown, as was his faded pants that were held up by suspenders over a torn and tattered dirty-white union suit with a patched flannel shirt layered over the top of that, partway unbuttoned down the front. The woodsman looked like he could use a good bath and flea dipping. His beard was dirty yellow and turning white. He was friendly with Cappie and often stopped by to visit and drop off a sample of his moonshine. A large well-honed knife was attached to his belt, and he carried a rifle in one hand and a mason jar filled with corn liquor in the other. He was looking for Cappie.

"Evening, gentlemen," he said. "I saw the light, and I thought maybe Cappie was back. I brought him a jar of my shine. My name's Jonah Flint. Would you mind holstering that Peacemaker, mister, before it goes off and hurts somebody?"

Nevada slowly holstered his gun when he saw there was no threat.

"Ooh, shine! We would be happy to take care of that for him," said Nevada, reaching for the mason jar.

Smokey gave Nevada a scornful look and then looked at the jar. *Up until this minute, I was doing a good job keeping Nevada away from the bars and the liquor bottles,* thought Smokey. *Nevada's new wife, Ricki, will get pissed if he starts hard drinking again.* Nevada's drinking problem started when he got himself roostered out on the desert, trying to poison himself with rotgut whiskey. Nevada never could get over the loss of his first sweetheart, Polly, and, at that time, turned to liquor for his salvation.

"Do you know where Cappie is, Jonah?" Smokey inquired.

"No. He's been gone for a couple of days, and it ain't like him to go without his pack horses and weapons. Who are you boys?"

"We are good friends of his. We came here to go hunting with him this week. He wasn't expecting us. We were going to surprise him," said Smokey. "I'm Smokey, and this here is Nevada."

"Oh, I heard Cappie tell of you two. He talked about you two a lot. I'm worried about him because there has been a lot of poaching on Cappie's traps this winter. He was going to try and catch the poachers. I'm hoping the poachers didn't catch him first and do harm to him."

"Why do you say that?" asked Nevada.

"Well, because they killed a trapper on the other side of this mountain just last week. I was worried they would get around to Cappie with the same violence."

"This sounds serious," said Nevada. "Now I know I'm going to follow those wagon tracks tomorrow morning. Do you know if Cappie owned a wagon?"

"No, he never owned a wagon. But I heard tell that the poachers had a wagon."

"This scene is getting worse by the minute. I got a real bad feeling," said Nevada.

"What is the closest town to here going down the other side of this mountain?" asked Smokey.

"Well now, that would be Harshaw. It's a mining town with a Spanish padre and some Mexicans. It was a boomtown, but now there is less than two hundred people living there. The gold mine played out. People keep leaving every day. It's a lawless town."

"Anything else we need to know about this town before we go there?" inquired Nevada. "Like, who is the sheriff?"

"There is no sheriff. It is patrolled by a United States circuit marshal once a month, and he doesn't stay long."

Nevada and Smokey exchanged glances with each other.

"You wouldn't happen to know when he was last in town, do you?" Nevada was very interested in the pattern of the law enforcement officer. He wasn't taking any more chances on brushes with the law. A few wanted posters on Nevada and Smokey might still be lurking out there somewhere, even though they did their time. You never know about these things. Word of apprehension doesn't always make it out to the distant towns and villages in the mountains. They would have to be very careful and watch their backs when they first enter the town.

"He usually shows the end of the month," replied Jonah.

"So we bought us some time on this one," said Smokey. "We maybe got ourselves about two weeks to get in there, find Cappie, and get the hell out of there."

"I'll tell you what, Jonah. I'll give you ten bucks, and you take care of Cappie's cabin, the three pack horses, and our personal belongings until we get back here, hopefully with Cappie. Is that a deal?"

"Yes, I will be happy to do that for you men and for Cappie. I can use your ten bucks."

"Good, Jonah. Smokey and I will leave at daybreak. Now how about the three of us having a shot of that shine of yours to seal the deal?"

"Sounds good to me," said Jonah. "Let me know what you think of it!"

Smokey started coughing after the first sip. Nevada laughed at him after taking his first sip. "It's strong stuff all right," said Nevada. "But it's real good."

"I might've known you would say that," replied Smokey.

Nevada just licked his lips and laughed. "Is this one-hundred proof?" he asked.

"I guess it's more like ninety-five," said Jonah. "A hundred proof would kill you."

"Ninety-five just about killed me," replied Smokey. "That shit's strong enough to make a jackrabbit spit in a bobcat's eye." Nevada laughed at Smokey. "I ain't kidding you, Nevada," said Smokey, "that stuff will make yuh see double an' feel single. Jonah, how do you keep a cork in that hooch?"

"Oh, I've had a few of them explode out of a bottle on me." Jonah laughed.

"What do you say we play a couple rounds of cards before we turn in for the night?" said Nevada.

"Sounds like a plan," said Smokey. "Jonah, do you play cards?"

"Sure, I do, but not for money. I ain't that good," replied Jonah.

"That's okay, Jonah. We aren't playing for money, just for fun. We could use matchsticks," said Nevada.

The three of them sat down and played several hands of cards then turned in when they got tired.

CHAPTER III

THE SEARCH

Early next morning, the Nevada Kid and Smokey followed the wagon and horse tracks down the other side of the mountain. The day was cloudy and overcast, but the clouds were moving on a slight breeze to the east. The harsh *char* notes of the cactus wren could be heard as they walked the horses along slowly. It was almost an entire day of traveling by horseback when they finally reached the run-down mining town of Harshaw. Gold Diggers Saloon and Gaming Hall was the first building at the edge of town, followed by an assay office, then a small bank, the general mercantile, the empty sheriff's office, a bookseller, another smaller general store, a barber shop, and a cafe. On the other side of the street were two more saloons, a rooming house with chickens running around in front of it, and a couple of brothels—one looked clean; the other looked rather dirty. They walked their horses up the main street, and Nevada glanced at Smokey with that serious look of his, and one corner of his lip curled up.

"I know," said Smokey. "It's got the same look as Chloride, doesn't it, pard?"

"Hell yeah!" Nevada answered.

"I told you all these mining towns looked alike."

"Do you think you can stay out of trouble so I don't have to bail you out or break you out of jail this time?" inquired Nevada.

21

"I think I can do better this time with no town sheriff. I learned my lesson in Chloride. Besides, we are on a mission for Cappie."

"See that you remember that," said Nevada.

"Let's check out the saloon," said Smokey.

"No, not yet. I want to go into here first." Nevada tried the door of the sheriff's office, and just as he thought, it was not locked. He walked in and looked around. The lock on the gun rack was broken, no guns or ammo in the office. It was probably looted sometime ago. A desk with scattered papers withering and tattered sat there against one wall, and he automatically checked through the wanted posters that were hanging on the wall and then went into the desk drawers, checking out some more older wanted posters. Nothing on himself, but there was an outdated wanted poster on Smokey. Nevada held it up in front of Smokey's face, and Smokey's eyes widened at its sight. Nevada balled it up, put a match to it, and used it to start a fire in the old wood stove. Against the wall was a set of bunk beds and some blankets. Wooden shutters on the single window in the room were closed and latched against the black window bars. The floor could use a good sweeping out. The coffeepot on the potbellied stove was clean and ready for its next use. Two old wooden chairs were in the corner near the stove. A small shelf on the wall had pegs under it with three coffee cups hanging on the pegs; one cup had chips in it. Nevada turned to Smokey. "We are sleeping in here tonight," he said as he checked that the front door had a good lock on it.

"Nevada! Are you crazy?" replied Smokey. *"In the sheriff's office? Really?"* This surprise was as unexpected as a fifth ace in a poker deck.

"Sure, why not? I don't expect anybody to bother us in this place. None of the characters in this town would even think of sleeping in the jailhouse. Besides, you know I'm not sleeping in another roach-infested hotel like the one in Chloride."

"This may be your idea of a fitting place to sleep, compadre, but not mine," said Smokey. He had all he could do to stop panting and swear a little.

"Well, you know where to find me if you want me." Nevada began unpacking his horse and bringing in what little they had in the way of personal belongings, dropping them on the lower bunk. He pulled coffee beans out of his saddlebags. He filled the coffeepot with water from the drinking barrel in the corner and put it back on the stove. Putting the beans into a piece of cheesecloth from his saddlebags and tying the cheesecloth, he dropped the beans into the pot. Then he added more wood to the stove, making it hotter so he was able to brew a fresh pot of hot coffee. "As soon as I have a fresh cup of coffee, we will go and check out the saloons," he said. "I can't survive without coffee to keep my reflexes fast."

Smokey just couldn't believe that Nevada had the balls and the brass to sleep in the sheriff's private office. Just then a Mexican wandered into the office. He was about five feet eight inches tall, had dark hair and black eyes, as black as the ace of spades. His belly was as big and as round as a wine barrel. His clothes were embroidered very fancily and colorfully. He wore spurs that jingled and a large sombrero hat tied under his fat chin so tightly it made a welt on his skin. He was clean-shaven, but his eyebrows were so thick they made a straight line across his forehead. His breath smelled of strong chewing tobacco.

"Gringos, what are you doing in here?" he questioned.

"We are sleeping in here tonight, my friend," said Nevada, sipping his coffee.

"But I am the mayor of this town, senors, and I am not exactly your friend. You cannot sleep in here. It is the sheriff's office."

"Do you have a sheriff? Is he here?" questioned Nevada.

"Well, no, senor. There is no sheriff here right now."

"Okay, Mr. Mayor. Here's five bucks for the town treasury. We are sleeping in here for the night. No more rooms at the hotel. You got any more problems with that?" Nevada's voice sounded menacing and stern. He took another sip of the strong black coffee.

"No. No problems, senor. But I know there are still rooms at the hotel. Thank you for the money, senor. I guess it will be okay for one night, if that is your choice. Especially since you are paying for the night."

"That is our choice. We will sleep in here tonight, Senor Mayor."

"Sí, senor." The mayor walked away feeling a little bit bewildered. But he wasn't any more confused than Smokey was feeling. Nevada picked up the broom and started sweeping some of the dirt and pieces of sagebrush out the office door. He put the broom back in the corner, finished the cup of coffee, and set down the cup.

"Now that we got that settled, Smokey, let's go get a look-see at that bar." Nevada took the front-door key from the nail on the door molding, and they locked the door on their way out.

"Boy, I'll tell you what, Nevada," said Smokey.

"*What?*" said Nevada with turbulence.

"Never mind. Nothing," said Smokey, shaking his head in disbelief as to what just happened. *How the hell did Nevada get away with the mayor letting him sleep in the sheriff's office?* he thought. He was scratching his head, still trying to figure that one out.

They walked down the wooden boardwalk to the Gold Diggers Saloon and Gaming Hall. The batwing doors creaked as they pushed through them, alerting everyone in the room that someone was entering. The barroom seemed to quiet down to a whisper at the intrusion of the two gringos with the tied-down holsters and low-hanging guns on their hips.

"Barkeep, I'll have a beer. What are you having, Nevada?" said Smokey.

"You got any sarsaparilla" inquired Nevada.

"Nevada, I'm proud of you," said Smokey.

"Sí, senor," said the bartender.

"Then I'll have a glass of that. Hey, is that apple pie I see behind you on that counter?"

"Sí, senor."

"I'll have me a piece of that also. Wow, that looks good and fresh."

"Sí, senor. Rosita, she made it this morning, and she brings it often."

A Mexican got up from a table and walked up to Nevada. "What is this? The young American cowboy does not drink a man's drink?"

This Mexican was about five feet eleven inches tall, wore double guns and holsters crisscrossed across his large stomach, and his clothes were slightly worn. He looked like a man to be reckoned with, tough and threatening.

"I drink, compadre. I'm just not drinking right now, is all."

"Oh, I see. You want to look around and see who is here first. Are you looking to see someone you know, gringo? Is it a sweet senorita or a man, if I may ask?"

"Matter of fact, hell yeah. I'm looking for a man, a trapper friend of mine named Cappie. Anybody around here see a man in buckskins selling furs?" The whole room went into a dead silence. Smokey and Nevada locked glances with each other.

"Well, actually, senor, a man like that went through here a couple of days ago. We don't know where he went or where he was going. He did not say. We suspect he was with Pedro and his boys. That is all we know."

"So they left town?" inquired Nevada.

"Sí, sí, senor."

"Which way did they head out?"

"No one knows, senor. It would be best if you two just git on your horses and go back to where you came from, senor. It would be healthier that way. If you know what I mean, senor."

"I know exactly what you mean, but I'm not buying any of it," said Nevada.

"Senor, I am trying hard to be nice to you and save you a lot of trouble. It would be most wise if you just leave and go back to where you came from," advised the Mexican.

Nevada turned his back to the man and started eating his apple pie and sipping his sarsaparilla. He turned back to look at the Mexican. "It would be even nicer if we go back to where we came from with our good friend. You see, we are here to go hunting in the mountains with Cappie."

"Oh, now I see, senor. Your timing was a little bit off. He left without you. It is too bad, senor. It is sad you must go back home without any hunting."

"You are a little bit mistaken on that one too, *paco*. Our hunting trip is now postponed and has turned into a search party for our friend. *Now*, if anyone in here knows who may have taken our friend Cappie and which way they headed, it would be much healthier for *all* of you if one of you would just be kind enough to pass on that information to us. Do we have any takers on this one?"

A grubby-looking man in a beat-up sombrero at the table in the back stood up, fast-drawing his gun. Nevada cut him down faster, startling everyone in the room. "Now does anyone else have any objections to answering our questions?"

"Senor, you are a very fast gunman. We cannot give you the answers you want. Pedro and his men will kill us all. They are very mean outlaws, senor, and very dangerous men. Pedro is so tough he grows horns like *el toro*."

Nevada finished his pie and his drink. He slowly put down the fork on the plate and pushed the empty pie plate across the bar toward the bartender. "I suggest, amigo, that you pick up that dead man before he starts stinking and put him to bed with a pick and shovel. I don't like anyone fast-drawing on me, forcing me to defend myself. Let's go, Smokey. We will try that other bar across the street."

As they walked out of the bar and through the squeaky batwing doors, the dead body of the Mexican was being carried away. A few Mexicans followed them into the Lost Dutchmen Saloon across the street, as their interest in these two cowboys was picking up. Some Mexicans were playing instruments and singing songs, and this establishment seemed livelier than the last one. They moseyed up to the bar and ordered two beers this time. Nevada took a deep swig and set the mug down. He fashioned himself a cigarette, lit it and inhaled deeply and waited a second and exhaled hard. Smokey took a chaw of his tobacco, chewed, then spit into the spittoon under the bar, catching it dead center. Nevada turned to face the customers in the bar. He stood with his legs apart, made sure the leather thong on his gun was loose in the holster, and shook out his gun hand to loosen it up also.

"We are looking for information on a friend of ours. He is a fur trapper named Cappie, and he wears buckskin clothing. I understand he passed through this son-of-a-bitch town a couple of days ago. Is there anyone here that would like to tell me how many men he was with and which way he headed out from here?" There was complete silence in the saloon. Again Nevada and Smokey's eyes locked in a side glance.

"What's the matter with you stupid people?" said Smokey.

Then Nevada interjected, "If there is a man among you with *balls* enough to tell me in private the answers I'm looking for, I'll be in the sheriff's office all night." He finished his smoke and threw it on the floor, stamping down hard on it and tamping it out. Then he and Smokey finished their beers, threw money on the bar, and left the saloon without another incident.

They walked down the boardwalk, back to the sheriff's office. The coffeepot was still hot, and they each had another cup of black coffee. "Smokey, these tight-mouthed Mexicans are making my skin get up an' crawl all over me," said Nevada.

"I hear you, Nevada. These people are definitely scared of something or somebody. This eerie atmosphere will make the hair on a buffalo robe stand up."

Just then there was a knock on the door of the sheriff's office. Smokey opened the door, and a pretty senorita brushed past him quickly slipping in.

"Well, *hello*, senorita. Wow, are you a pretty one! What can we do for you, darlin'?" said Smokey. She was carrying a plate of tortillas for their supper and handed it to Nevada.

"Well, thank you, ma'am. Look, Smokey! Supper."

Rosita was a small and very pretty girl. Her long black hair was so shiny it almost looked like the polished blue steel of a gun barrel. She wore a red rose over one ear in her hair. Her cheekbones were high and had a peachy pink color to them, and she wore face powder to keep the shine from the day's heat from coming through and filling up her face with beads of perspiration. She was very petite at about four feet eleven in height. She had small hands and feet and rounded hips that made her small waistline look even smaller.

"Senors, my name is Rosita. I hear you are very fast gunmen and you are looking for your friend Cappie. I know Cappie personally. He is a good man, senors."

"Rosita," repeated Nevada. "Are you the same Rosita that bakes good apple pies?"

"Sí, senor. The saloon pays me to bake for them. It is a living."

"Wow! That was the best apple pie I ever ate at a bar. My compliments to you, ma'am. Thank you also for bringing us some supper. So what is it you know about our friend Cappie?"

"Cappie is a friend of mine also. He was taken through here two days ago by Pedro and his very bad men, senor. His hands were tied behind his back, and he was in their wagon. One of Pedro's vaqueros was riding Cappie's horse. I suspect they took him north into the mountains, where they have a hideout somewhere near the mining area, in a camp or in a cave."

"Did these bandits have a wagonful of furs with them?" questioned Nevada.

"Sí, senor. The furs were sold to various merchants in the area for pesos and duro. The wagon was left at the livery stable, and they switched Cappie onto a mule. It is suspected they took Cappie to their hideout in the mountains. Be careful, senor, if you go after them. They are very dangerous men."

"Thank you, senorita. I'm very beholden to you for the information and the good food," said Nevada. "We are going after them, but we will be careful."

"Are you going to save Cappie from these very evil outlaws, senor?" said Rosita.

"We will try our best, Rosita. Cappie is our compadre," said Nevada.

"Thank you, senors. I will be most grateful if you can bring him back safely." Rosita secretly left the sheriff's office and slipped away, back down the street to her casa or home. As she went out the door, they could hear the sound of a dog barking angrily down the street and a goat baaing back at it.

"She 'will be most grateful,'" repeated Smokey. "I wonder how grateful she intends to be if we bring Cappie back?" Nevada cast Smokey a look of disapproval.

"We will head out in the morning for the mountains, Smokey. Might as well spend one last night here. If we left now, we wouldn't get very far before we would have to make a night camp somewhere on the trail."

"Well, it's a little too early for bedtime. I'm heading down to that brothel I saw on the way in here. Those girls in the one place looked clean and didn't look too bad. You coming with me?"

"No. You went and got me married to Ricki last month. Remember the surprise wedding you planned for me? The one where everybody in Arizona knew I was getting married but me?"

"Oh yeah, that. You had to get married and settled down if you want to do that custody battle for your son, TJ. At least that is what the attorney, Mr. Parks, said. My plan was *not* to get you married but to start up a relationship again with you and Ricki. Ricki thought I meant you wanted to get married. Then the whole thing ricocheted out of control. When it got so far out of hand, I couldn't stop it."

"Well, I'm not complaining, and I'm not gonna cheat on Ricki. I had enough of wandering through brothels and messing with saloon girls. Maybe it's time for me to grow up and take life seriously now that I'm married and a property owner. I can wait until I get home to Ricki. She is worth waiting for. Besides, I had the clap once from a saloon girl, and no way in hell do I want to get that cure again."

"Well now, Nevada. You have turned out to be a real good boy, a solid citizen, and a responsible business owner. Suit yourself, buddy. I'll see you in the morning. It's going to be a boring night for you," said Smokey.

"Smokey, *stay out of trouble.*"

"I hear you, compadre," said Smokey.

I'm getting that bad feeling again, thought Nevada.

Smokey had no trouble picking out Carmelita in the cleaner brothel. She was the prettiest girl in the bawdy house, standing five feet three inches tall. Carmelita was well-endowed on the top, with a nice, evenly coordinated figure. Her skirt was bright red, and her blouse was white and ruffled off-the-shoulders style. Her slippers were soft, black Mary Jane style with a strap over the instep. She had a nice, clean room with the usual white lace curtains on a single window. The window was open five inches to air the room, and the curtains were blowing inward, fighting against a soft, sighing breeze. That soft breeze brought in with it the greasy smell of hot chili peppers frying somewhere in a nearby casa. A liquor bottle and two glasses sat on a nightstand next to the bed, beckoning anyone to take a drink. Jose Cuervo was written on the bottle, and the worm was still floating in the bottle, so it was fairly new. Carmelita pulled off Smokey's boots, and Smokey wasted no time pouring the drinks, unbuttoning the fly of his jeans, and taking them off along with his red long johns. He was in bed with her in no time at all. Remembering Nevada's warning, Smokey went light on the liquor but slow and heavy on the sex. It had been a while since he was with a woman as good-looking as this one. He was taking his time with the senorita and kissing her passionately, moving down to all her special spots. He pulled her against his hard chest then, with both hands, grabbed her butt and pulled her firmly against his hard manhood. He also liked touching her soft, full curved breasts, delighting in the beauty of her feminine body. Looking at the swelling and cleavage gave him a masculine feeling of dominance over her body. He continued to make love to her for a long time before satisfying both their needs for a good climax. Continuing to hold her in his arms after the climax, they relaxed from the delight of their lovemaking. Then suddenly the sound of a fist pounding on the outside of the door to her room startled them both out of their sweet, rechargeable moment.

"Carmelita, it is *Amado* Pedro. Open the door, or I will bust it down."

"Oh, *mamma mia*!" she screamed. "Pedro is back. He will kill you, senor, if he finds you in here with me! Pedro thinks he is my lover and my man. Go out the window quickly! I will stall him off. He is a very bad hombre."

"Shit," said Smokey. *Of all people, it's Pedro the Outlaw.* He quickly pulled on his pants, leaving his red union suit on the floor. Then he pulled on his boots, grabbed his shirt, and pulled it over his head, not stopping to button up the three buttons. Then Smokey snatched up his gun belt and sidearm and stepped through the window, carrying them instead of stopping to put them on. With his gun and holster in his hand, sliding down the roof, he jumped down onto the boardwalk, right into the grasp of a group Pedro's ornery-looking men.

"Hombre, what are you doing coming out of Carmelita's window? When Pedro finds out, Pedro will not like this at all," said a husky Mexican. "Pedro will be very mad. I shall have to tell him."

30

"Oh shit," said Smokey again.

They took his gun and holster and tied his hands behind him. Smokey took off running up the boardwalk with his hands tied behind him, straight toward the sheriff's office. Stray bullets fired in the air as warning shots were missing him, coming from behind. The unruly gang of outlaws followed him up the boardwalk. Smokey stopped at the sheriff's office and was screaming and kicking at the door for Nevada to unlock it.

Nevada awoke suddenly to the screaming voice of Smokey and unlocked the door, opening it in time to let the whole outlaw gang in through the door at two in the morning.

"What is this?" said the husky Mexican. "We have not one but two hombres. They are in here, bunking in the good sheriff's office."

They subdued a sleepy-eyed Nevada, tying his hands behind his back also. Then, in the next instant, in walked Pedro. He smacked Smokey backhanded across the face, cutting the corner of his lip.

"Hey, gringo. You forgot your drawers." Pedro pitched the red union suit on the floor of the sheriff's office. "So you like making love to my girl, Carmelita, huh?" he said to Smokey. "Well, it will be your last time, senor. Because I shall have to shoot off your cojones and kill you to teach Carmelita a lesson for cheating on me again," said Pedro.

"Oh shit," replied Smokey.

Nevada, in his waking twilight moment, was just now figuring out what was going on and coming on down, so he rolled his eyes up to the ceiling, shaking his head. "Smokey, I told you to stay out of trouble. Geez!"

Smokey just said, "Sorry, boss."

"Two of you stay here and guard them till morning. I will have my evening with Carmelita, and then later in the morning, we will head back up the mountains," said Pedro.

Nevada and Smokey slept sitting up on the lower bunk with their hands tied behind their backs. It was not a comfortable position for a good night's sleep, and Nevada was getting pissed off because his wrists were getting burned and sore from trying to release and loosen the ropes. His body parts that were bruised and broken from working the rodeo circuit were aching and sore. His arms were feeling as limp as a neck-wrung rooster, and his long legs felt weak like worn-out fiddle strings.

When dawn finally broke through the morning clouds, the outlaws were getting the horses saddled and ready for their trip back into the mountains. The two American cowboys were ushered out to the boardwalk at gunpoint and told to mount their horses. The band of outlaws headed north out of town, toward the mountains. Nevada noticed one of the vaqueros was riding Cappie's horse, Wolfe. This did not sit well with him. He locked gazes with Smokey's eyes and looked back at the horse then back to Smokey again. Smokey's eyes indicated that he got the message.

They followed an old Apache Indian trail into the mountains, passing giant ponderosa pine and large saguaro cacti. As they wove between small spires of rock, the terrain began to get rougher with volcanic rock formations. Then came towering mountain peaks and very deep canyons as they continued to climb. They were nearing the sacred grounds of the Indians, home to their thunder god. As they continued on the trail for another couple of miles, two mule deer caught their movement and noise, scurrying away from them as far as they could go. A bobcat in the trail, hunting for its breakfast, was surprised by the group of horses coming at it, and it hissed and growled as it cowered, startling the horses. A bandit shot it with his gun, silencing its insolence forever. Ferns were growing along the trail, giving it a soft, woodsy look as the horses walked by, passing the thick underbrush of the wooded trail. Mesquite trees interspersed with white cedar offered shade along the narrow trail.

They branched off from the main trail and crossed some rugged terrain for about a mile, heading toward an old abandoned Apache Indian camp and an abandoned cave with a mine shaft of some kind that was started and never finished. An Apache longhouse in the camp area was still useful for a shelter, and the outlaws seemed to be taking advantage of it. Evidently they had reached their destination, because they were dismounting and unsaddling the horses. A corral for the horses was previously formed by the Indians using thick dried vines gathered from the underbrush of the desert vegetation and woven into a circle, fencing in the horses, grouping them in a rustic corral. It was a rugged, temporary camp and was nothing like the outlaw camp of the Cole Younger Gang that Nevada and Smokey lived in for over a year and a half. In fact, the Younger Brothers' camp was a palace compared to this one.

Two of the bandits came over to Nevada and Smokey and pulled them down off their horses. They checked that the cowboys' hands were still tied behind them. They walked them over near the cave and pushed them both into a hole, surprising the two cowboys. They hit bottom with a loud thump.

"Shit," said Smokey.

"Ow! My bad leg," said Nevada. Nevada looked up to the top of the hole. It looked to be about eight to ten feet deep, maybe more, and may be some kind of mine shaft from an old abandoned gold mine. The mine's shaft was only partially dug out, and it was never finished because no tunnels ran off from it. "Boy, are we in deep shit," murmured Nevada.

"Hey, Nevada," said Smokey. "There's somebody else down here." They struggled over to the other side of the pit to look at an unconscious figure curled up on the ground in a fetal position. "It's Cappie! We found him the hard way," said Smokey.

"No," said Nevada. "We found him the easy way. They brought us right to him. We would never have known to leave the trail and find this abandoned Indian camp. It would have taken us days to find this spot and track Cappie here to this hole in the ground." A little sunlight was shining down into the shaft, giving them just enough light to see beyond the shadows.

"He is not in good shape, Nevada. He was beat up, and he is unconscious. This is not looking good at all. We can't even help ourselves with our hands tied behind our backs. How can we help him? You got any of your wisdom on this one?"

"Only one idea, but it's not gonna get us out of this dark hole in the ground. I have a penknife in my right boot, on the inside seam. When I worked in the tack shop, I fashioned a little holster type of pocket to hold my knife inside my boot. I can't reach it, though, with my hands tied behind my back."

"No shit? A knife?" said Smokey. "Can we cut these ropes somehow?"

"Hell yeah. I have an idea. You sit on the ground. I'll lie on the ground and move around behind you and try and position my right boot up against your tied hands. See if you can get your fingers into my boot and pull out the knife. Be careful, there is a release on the side of the knife. It *will* snap open very fast. Cut your ropes, then cut mine. At least our hands will be free, and we can cut the ropes that are tying Cappie's hands also."

It was a struggle for Smokey to get his long fingers into Nevada's boot. However, they had a lot of time to work at it, and they were not in any hurry since they were not going anywhere anytime soon.

"I got it, Nevada! I got hold of the knife, and I can feel the pin that snaps it open. There it is! Okay, now let's see if I can cut these ropes. Shit. This blade is honed sharp."

"Did you get cut?" replied Nevada.

"No, but damn close. It's coming good. I got it!"

"Shhh. Not so loud. They will hear you," said Nevada.

Smokey slipped behind Nevada and cut his hands free and then moved over to Cappie and cut the ropes binding his hands also. He handed Nevada his knife back, and Nevada closed it, putting it back in his boot.

Nevada found his matches in a pocket in his black leather vest. "They took my tobacco and makings but missed my matches." He sparked a match against his empty holster. The mine shaft lit up like daylight, and they could see where they were. He gathered up all the pieces of rope. Cappie's roping was the longest piece, and he threw them over to Smokey. "Knot them pieces all together in one long rope. I don't know if we will get any use out of it, but at least we have something, even if it's too short."

"Okay, Nevada," replied Smokey.

Nevada held the match up high, looking at the top of the hole in the ground. "It's definitely eight to ten feet to the top." He had to extinguish the match before it burned his fingers. "It's too far above my head. I can't even jump up to the top and grab the edge."

"How about if you stood on my shoulders?"

"No, you could never hold all my weight. I can't hold your weight either with my bad leg. I have no strength in my left leg. We will figure this out later. Right now we got to see to Cappie."

"Well, we got about four and a half feet of rope. Not enough to do anything with," said Smokey.

Nevada sparked another match and slipped over to Cappie, lighting up his face. "He's still alive and breathing, but breathing shallow. He needs water and a blanket. He can't last more'n another day or maybe two. We gotta get them to throw down a canteen and some blankets."

"They don't look like the compassionate type of outlaws," replied Smokey.

"Smokey, you are a good con artist. Call them over and see if you can con anything out of them—food, water, or a blanket."

"Hey, you pepper-gut sons-of-bitches," called Smokey.

"Be nice. You ain't gettin' nothing out of them that way." Nevada laughed.

"It's the only language they understand," replied Smokey.

"Hey, senors!" yelled Nevada. "Hey, you up there."

"Sí, senors. You hombres calling for us?"

"Yes. We need water down here bad. How about a canteen, some blankets, and something to eat? It is barbaric to leave men down here in a hole without anything. Where are your manners, my friends?" said Nevada.

"Pedro has not approved that as yet, senors."

"C'mon, we need help down here. I would not do this to you, my friend," replied Nevada.

"Okay, I will throw a canteen down, gringo. But how you will drink it in the dark and with your hands tied, I know not, senors."

"Just throw it down, and we will figure it out, my friend," said Nevada.

A couple of minutes passed, and a canteen full of water came crashing down into the shaft, bouncing off the side wall, almost hitting Nevada. His quick reflexes caught it before it hit the ground.

"Thank you, my friend," said Nevada. He quickly took a sip and handed it to Smokey, who took a good drink. He handed it back to Nevada, and

Nevada quickly went over to Cappie and tried to revive him, giving him a sip of cold water. He took off his bandana and wet it down, washing Cappie's face with it. Suddenly Cappie came to and opened his eyes. There was fear in those eyes. "Relax, Cappie. It's Nevada. Smokey and I are down in this mine hole with you."

"Where in the hell did you two spring up from?" questioned Cappie.

"Well, it started out being a surprise visit to your cabin for a hunting trip. Then it became a search party for you. Now it has become a prison escape plan for the three of us."

"Sounds a little complicated to me," said Cappie.

"It's getting worse by the minute," replied Nevada. "Are you gonna be okay?"

"I think they broke my arm, Nevada, when they threw me down in this old abandoned mine shaft. I can't move it."

"I told you it's getting worse by the minute. Smokey, come over here and look at his arm. What do you think?"

"Can you move it this way, Cappie?"

"Hell no," said Cappie. "Ow! That's painful."

"It's broken all right, Nevada," said Smokey.

"Is there anything we can do for it?" questioned Nevada.

"Well, I can set it and then use these pieces of rope to tie it up in a makeshift sling. At least it will heal properly until we can get out of here and get him to a doctor."

"Do you know how to set it?" queried Nevada.

"Hell yeah. I watched it done a couple times in Union camps when I was scouting for the Union Army during the war. I know how to position it for the set, but I'm not sure if I have the strength to set it right."

"Well then, let's do it. Give it a try for now," said Nevada. "If I strike a match and hold it up for you, can you try to set it for him?

"Sure, but don't strike the match until I tell you to. No sense wasting the matches. I'll tell you when to strike it," said Smokey.

"Okay, Cappie. I want you to hold your arm in this position. Don't move now. Now strike the match, Nevada." Nevada struck the match and held it while Smokey pulled the arm into place, setting it. He could tell in the light that it went in correctly when Cappie yelled out in pain. "Okay, I got it set. Now light another match, and I will fashion a temporary rope sling. But I got to see what it is I'm doing. Okay, strike the match now, Nevada."

"I'm running low on matches."

"It's okay, Nevada. I'm about done. How does that feel, Cappie?"

"Actually, its feels less painful like this."

"Good, then I did everything right," replied Smokey.

Nevada handed the canteen to Cappie. "Take a good drink of water, Cappie. You were dehydrated when we found you."

"Thanks, Nevada. You two boys are lifesavers."

"Well, that remains to be seen. We are all still in trouble together. We gotta get out of this half hole of a mining shaft. As long as we are all stuck down here, you wanna tell us exactly what happened? These Mexicans have been poaching your traps all winter? That's what Jonah the Moonshiner said."

"Yes, Nevada," replied Cappie. "They have been stealing the furs out of my traps and selling them everywhere to get extra money for supplies and ammunition. I caught them one afternoon, and there were too many of them for me to take on. They just seemed to leak out of the wooded landscape from everywhere. They tied me up, stole all my furs from the cabin, and took off with me in the wagon. They also stole my horse, Wolfe. I thought I was a goner. Then they threw me into this old half dugout and abandoned mine shaft. They roughed me up quite a bit before dropping me down here. I must have blacked out when I hit bottom and broke my arm. I don't know how long I have been down in this hole."

"My guess is this will probably be about the third day," said Nevada. "Smokey and I have been here about a half day. We are cold, hungry, and we want to get the hell out of here fast. Besides, I'm getting real pissed off."

"Nevada," said Smokey. "You got to use that wit of yours and figure out how to get us out of here. You have always been good in tight situations."

"This is different, Smokey. I can't reach the rim of this hole. Even if I stand on your shoulders, I can't reach it. I'm beginning to feel dizzy, like these walls are closing in on me. I never knew I was claustrophobic until now."

"Hey, *paco*! Can anybody hear me up there?" hollered Nevada.

"Sí, senor. You seem to have a lot of problems down there. I keep hearing screaming noises. Hombre, what is your trouble now?"

"We are freezing down here. Throw down a couple of blankets. We got a sick man down here with us. This is not right, senor. We want better treatment."

"You will not need blankets by tomorrow, hombre. You will be killed in the afternoon."

"Well, then my last request is blankets, *paco*. How about it, my friend?"

"If Pedro approves it, I will send some down, senor."

"These idiots are getting on my nerves," said Nevada. "If I get out of this hole, I'll kick their asses so far it will take a bloodhound six weeks to find their smell!"

"Calm down, Nevada. You're dander is beginning to show." Smokey laughed.

"Oh yeah, when I get back up on that flat ground, these chili-eaters are gonna know how gruff my constitution can get."

Suddenly, three wool blankets came flying down the mine shaft, landing on the dirt floor in front of them. "Hombres, there will be no more requests. Pedro says you will all die tomorrow afternoon, and there will be no more requests out of you."

"We shall see about that," answered Nevada.

They took the wool blankets and wrapped one around Cappie and taking one each of the other two blankets, wrapping them around themselves. Then they pulled Cappie up in between them to keep him warm, protecting him with the heat from their own bodies.

Exhausted from the experience of the day, they fell asleep huddled together, sleeping very soundly. Nevada said a silent prayer that it wouldn't snow or rain with a sudden temperature drop in these mountains tonight, or they were in even bigger trouble down in this hole.

The morning sunlight flickering in the shadows woke the three prisoners up, and Nevada's temperament was building up even worse than it was the night before.

"Damn! I'm hungry, and I don't like being hungry." Nevada had a pretty good grouch going on.

"Take it easy, kid," said Smokey. "I know you are a growing boy and need your nourishment. We're hungry too. Us older boys can go hungry a little longer than you young pups. We have more tolerance."

"Screw tolerance and fuck them bastards," said Nevada. "I need something for breakfast. I got to get out of this here hole now before I starve to death."

Smokey handed Nevada the canteen of water. "Drink water. It will help with the hunger pains, kid."

"I'd rather have a glass of eighty-proof sipping tequila on the rocks," said Nevada. "Or even better, some of Jonah's ninety-five-proof shine."

"Well, you are out of luck, kid, because we don't have any," said Smokey.

Cappie just shook his head. Watching these two cowboys was like watching a vaudeville act on the stage of the Old Opera House. The more Smokey tried to calm down Nevada's horn-tossing mood, the more frothy a rise would come out of him.

"Calm down, you two, it sounds like these outlaws are leaving the camp. I hear horses riding away. Listen a minute," said Cappie.

"You're right, Cappie. They're leaving. I need a good shot of something to calm my nerves," replied Nevada.

"I'll give you a good shot of something from the end of my right fist, Nevada. Now calm down and use your wits to think of a way to get us out of here," said Smokey. "You are the only one here with enough sand in you to do that."

"I've plum run out of damn ideas," said Nevada.

CHAPTER IV

THE RESCUE

Keytoe was a half-breed Apache Indian. His mother was Apache Indian, and his father was a mountain man. He was only fifteen years old, but the bloodline he came from was all frontier born and bred. His eyes were as black and shiny, as was his long, shoulder-length, straight, silky black hair. He was slim and muscular, and his body was built rock hard. Keytoe was keeping an eye on these Mexicans who were invading the sacred lands of the Apache thunder god, and he was not happy about the trespassing. He would occasionally stop by the outlaw camp when he came down from his hut in the mountains to hunt for his food and provide for his survival and the survival of his mother and family tribal members. Now he noticed not just one man was being held in the mine shaft, but now the Mexican outlaws were holding three American prisoners. If these men were not released soon, they would all die. He was not sure what he could do about it, if anything. Keytoe figured he would stalk the camp and wait it out for a while to see what would happen. He decided to go back to the small mine entrance he found yesterday and sleep the night there, returning in the morning to scout the camp some more.

When morning dawned, the arid mountain air was dry and thirsty for water. The plants and animals of the area were adapted to the conditions, as well as Keytoe, the Indian boy. He took a drink of water from his skin pouch. His breakfast was a rabbit he snared in a trap during the night. After satisfying his hunger, he decided to check out the outlaw camp once more. To his surprise, the outlaws were heading down the mountain, back toward the town of Harshaw, leaving only two guards watching over the camp. This was going to be easier than he originally thought. He snuck up on the first guard and killed him, stabbing him in the back with his sharp hunting knife. The second guard met the same fate. He slipped over to the corral and snatched some ropes and a horse, leading the horse over to the hole in the ground.

He called down into the mine shaft to the three men. No answer. He called down again, and there was some stirring of bodies moving around and whispering.

Smokey looked up at what he thought was the sound of a voice coming from up above just as Keytoe's arrow struck the ground at their feet.

"Shit! Nevada. Now it's Indians!" screamed Smokey.

"What?" replied Nevada. "Indians? That's all we need now." He picked up the arrow and looked at it. Cappie took the arrow from Nevada's hand and looked at it.

"These are friendly Apache Indians. I'm familiar with the marking on this kind of arrow."

"Hello!" Keytoe called down to them. "Watch your heads. I'm throwing down a rope." He threw down a rope that he had knotted in perfect fashion for climbing out of the hole. One end of the rope was tied to the standing horse that Keytoe was holding on to. Nevada took it immediately and climbed up the rope using the knots as a ladder to get him to the surface, struggling to get out at the top. Keytoe helped him get out the rest of the way.

Nevada noticed the rope was looped over the horse for support. "You speak English?" said Nevada. "You did a good job, son."

"Yes. My father was a mountain man. My mother is Apache Indian. Let's get these American men out before the outlaws come back." Nevada looked around the camp and noticed two dead outlaw sentries from knife wounds. *What a break*, he thought. *This Indian boy did better than just a good job. He did great!*

"We have a wounded man down there," he said to Keytoe. "We will tie the rope around him and let the horse pull him up first."

"That will work, but hurry," said Keytoe.

Smokey tied the rope around Cappie, securing it well, and they slowly backed up the horse, pulling Cappie up to the top of the mine shaft and out of the hole when he reached the top. Then the rope was sent back down the shaft to Smokey, and he climbed up the knots the same way Nevada did it.

"I'm called Keytoe. I live on top of this mountain. This camp is on the sacred ground of our thunder god. These men do not belong here. I have been watching them for days now." They all shook hands with the young Indian boy, Keytoe. They let Cappie lie and rest for a minute so he could catch his breath.

"Put Cappie on his horse, and let's get the hell off this mountain," said Nevada.

"No," said Keytoe. "We must go up the mountain, not down. If you go down, you will run into camp guards and maybe the outlaws coming back up. There is only one trail. I have a camp in the mountains where I live, and I will take you there. But we must walk there. You cannot take a horse up there in these rocks. You will kill the horse."

"Shit," said Cappie. "I've got to leave Wolfe here with these son-of-a-bitch pepper-guts?"

"We have no choice, Cappie. Smokey and I have to leave Jawbone and Tacco here also. Guess there's just no other option," said Nevada. "Lead the way, Keytoe. Get us the hell out of here. I don't want to wind up back in that hole for another night."

They retrieved their guns and rifles from their saddles before leaving camp. Nevada tossed Keytoe an extra rifle and box of shells for himself. Keytoe was quite surprised and caught it the instant it came flying through the air.

Nevada and Smokey each helped support Cappie and helped lead him across the rocky area heading up the slope of the mountain, following Keytoe upward through the vegetation.

They stopped at the abandoned mine shaft where Keytoe slept the night before, giving Cappie a rest so he could catch his breath. Keytoe offered them all a drink of water from his skin pouch. They continued up the mountain until they came to a small brook where Keytoe refilled his water pouch in a small waterfall seeping down through the rocks into a rushing brook that was five feet across. Nevada could see crayfish moving across rocks and tiny minnows darting up and down the brook through the crystal-clear water. *Wow!* he thought. *Mother Nature's silent whispering at its best. I can just tell this is Indian country. The natural forest floor has not been disturbed.*

This area of the mountain was pristine land, untouched by the white man and civilization. This was all land held sacred by the Indian tribes. Its beauty cannot even be captured in a serious painting. They continued walking on a zigzagging path through the rocks and spires, avoiding the larger boulders and crevices where snakes may be hiding. Keytoe seemed to know exactly where he was heading. No wonder the horses could not come. Keytoe knew this terrain like a map in his hand. It was not likely any of the outlaws would attempt to wander this far up in these rocks. Keytoe led them on a sudden turn off the rocky trail and through a flat area totally covered with ferns and fairy dusters then on through woody plants like desert mistletoe, brittlebush, limber bush, and on into a small clearing that looked out from the mountainside. In this small clearing were several small beehive-looking huts built by Keytoe's Indian tribe as a small encampment. He led the three men to a lodge belonging to his mother, a widowed Indian squaw. A campfire was glowing in the center of the hut, and Keytoe's mother was cooking a daily meal. She was not surprised when

Keytoe came in leading three American men into her lodge. Nevada looked around at the structure of the hut with its framework of heavy poles but sheathed only with grass thatching. It was suited for the warmer climates of the South. The thatching was tied down by slender wooden rods or roots that were easy to bend and tie down in a weaving pattern.

These Indians were toughened to the extremes of life lived close to nature. They traveled under the harsh sun in summer and worked outdoors in winter. Young boys of five or six years owned their own horses and were good riders, able to herd horses. Young girls of the same age would dig roots and carry water and wood.

"Mother," said Keytoe, "these are the American men I told you about that were held hostage down in the mine shaft. The outlaws left camp for the morning, and I was able to get them out."

"You are a good son," she said. "You have all the makings of your father." She immediately busied herself with boiling herbs to give to Cappie for his pain. Checking his broken arm, she could see that it was properly set and replaced the knotted worn ropes with leather lacing and a deerskin sling. The three men lay down on the deerskin mats to rest and get some much-needed sleep. They were awakened by Keytoe around dusk to eat some supper, which Cameo, Keytoe's mother, had cooked for them. Keytoe's father nicknamed his wife Cameo after a piece of jewelry he brought back for her from a small-town mercantile where he traded his animal hides.

Now that Keytoe's father was killed by outlaws, Keytoe was the head and the boss of his mother's household. Cameo lived a satisfying, self-respecting life. The women in this camp outnumbered the men because many of the men were killed and chased from their lands, dying at war, fighting the white man. The men that were left had to take more than one wife because there were so many widows. Some Indians believed this was proper; some did not. These Indians had a way of life that was dominated by religion and respect for their thunder god. In another year, when Keytoe was sixteen, it would be time for him to start looking for a wife to share his life. It would be his choice alone to have more than one. When Keytoe explained this custom to Cappie and the two cowboys that evening, the giggles around the campfire were turning into laughter.

"Ricki is such a spitfire I got all I can do to handle her," replied Nevada. "I can't imagine pleasing more than one of her."

"Why do you think Cappie and I are still single?" Smokey laughed. "Although you were doing pretty good, Nevada, at keeping it all straight when you had half-a-dozen saloon girls chasing you at the same time a few months back!"

"Maybe that's why I decided to ask for Ricki's hand in marriage. It was beginning to be intolerable for me. I was starting to call the girls by their wrong names and got my face slapped more than once!" Laughter resounded throughout the hut. Even Cameo smiled and silently giggled, finding it amusing. "Well, what could I do? After drinking all night, I wasn't sure, after a while, who I was talking to!" More laughter a little louder this time.

"It is time to bed down for the night, my new friends," said Keytoe. "My mother and I will sleep in my grandmother's hut for tonight. This will give you the peace and quiet of your own hut. Come, Mother. I will help you carry your belongings."

"Good night, Keytoe. Thank you both for everything," said Nevada.

"Yeah, we sure do appreciate it," replied Smokey.

Chapter V

HUNT FOR SURVIVAL

Morning came quickly in the little Indian encampment, and everyone was busy getting the breakfast prepared. The hustle and bustle of the encampment woke up the two cowboys and Cappie, who realized that it was not altogether different than waking up in a busy cow camp on a cattle drive. Rabbit stew was passed around, and the men seemed to be eating first while the women and children waited for the men to be finished. Then it was time for the rest of the camp to eat.

The men were getting ready to go hunting for game as they gathered their bows and arrows, preparing to leave the camp. They were leaving in groups of twos and threes. Keytoe came up to Nevada and Smokey. "It is time to replenish fresh game for the camp. Our supplies are almost gone," said Keytoe. "Are you two cowboys interested in hunting?"

"I am," Nevada answered quickly. "Especially since we ate your food last night."

"Me too," said Smokey. "That's what we originally came here for, hunting."

"Cappie will have to stay here and get well. My mother will take care of him. He must be well and strong to make the trip back home when I lead you back down the mountain tomorrow," said Keytoe.

"Sounds like good advice," said Nevada. "We'll be back for you, Cappie. See you later on."

Keytoe, Nevada, and Smokey climbed up the rocky mountain for about two hours. When they were about five thousand feet up, they were in the snow line and ahead of the thicker part of the tree line. Mule-deer tracks were being spotted around the slopes and heading toward a valley. The air higher in the mountains was cool and crisp, but their excitement was high. The cowboys loved big-game hunting because the unexpected always seemed to happen. This time it would be more exciting than they thought, because they borrowed bows and arrows from the Indians for the hunt. They could not take a chance on rifle fire alerting the outlaws of their presence on the upper slopes of the mountain. The Indian camp was in dire need of meat to get them through until the spring thaws arrived. They studied some tracks in the snow very carefully and decided it was probably a buck chasing a doe, so they decided to follow the tracks.

"Nevada, bucks have personalities, and what's more interesting is, those personalities can change from year to year. Sometimes it's easier to hunt an older buck, say six years old, because as they age, they are easier to kill," said Keytoe.

"That's very interesting, Keytoe. I'll remember that. Maybe that's why most bucks I shoot are older, and I usually get them at sundown, when they do dumb things that make them easier to get."

"That's right, Nevada. The older they get, the more they become comfortable and lazy, so they become more visible during the hunt. Today we are hunting buck that are daylight-active. Shhh. We are getting close," said Keytoe. "I will let you and Smokey shoot first, and I will back you up in case your arrows miss."

"Are you saying there is a good chance we will miss the target and you won't?" inquired Nevada with a grin.

"I'm saying we shall see who is the marksman." Keytoe laughed. "Have you ever shot a bow and arrow before?"

"No," said Smokey. "Neither one of us."

Keytoe giggled again.

"As a young farm boy, I shot plenty of moving targets using a slingshot and nuts," said Nevada.

"Nuts?" said Smokey. "I always thought you were a little squirrely."

"Hell yeah. I climbed the nut tree on the edge of the woods by the schoolyard. I would get high up in that tree and pick the nuts and shoot them one at a time with my slingshot at the ranch boys that were harassing me for being a farmer's son!"

"You were a vinegary kid, Nevada." Smokey laughed.

"I was ornery all right from so much harassment. But I'll tell you what. I made some real good slingshots over the years. I got a good whooping, though, with Pa's razor strap for hitting a horse with one of those nuts. The horse bolted, knocking a rancher's son off it, breaking the kid's leg."

"I never knew of anybody that could get into as much trouble as you without even trying." Smokey laughed.

They noticed a muley buck about two hundred yards away and carefully and quietly made a stand. It was cropping the grass and not taking heed of its surroundings. All three arrows whined through the air in a row, one behind the other. Smokey's arrow was first and missed the buck, docking in a tree. Nevada's arrow caught the buck in the thigh, dropping it to one knee. Keytoe's arrow hit its mark dead center and killed the buck. This all happened simultaneously, as if it was one arrow shot. Keytoe was laughing hard in amusement at the two cowboys. They got the message. You cannot outshoot an Indian buck with bows and arrows no matter how hard you try. Keytoe was an ace with the bow and arrow, and he nailed that buck good.

The buck was field-dressed out, and they carried it back toward the camp, stopping along the way to gather some snared rabbits from Keytoe's traps. They arrived at the Indian camp near dusk, adding the catch from their hunt to the others that were being brought in by the Apache Indian bucks. The squaws were already skinning the hides and were preparing the meat and the hides to preserve them for the rest of the winter months. This day's hunt was a substantial gathering of meat provisions to get the tribe through the spring season meltdown.

As they sat around the campfire eating the evening meal, they were discussing the plans for the events of the next day. Cappie's strength was back, and he was joining in on the plans to return home to his cabin.

"We will first scout the outlaws' camp, and if the outlaws are still there, we will have to make plans to take them down," said Nevada. "We have our rifles, and now Keytoe has a rifle he can keep for his own. However, we will need all the men we can muster to clean out that nest of greasers."

"My braves will all work with us to get them out of our sacred lands," said Keytoe.

"How many braves do you have, Keytoe?" inquired Nevada.

"They are just young boys my age and younger, most of them under fifteen years. However, they are skilled bowmen. I can muster about ten or twelve. I will tell them to be ready to move out in the morning. They will feel proud to be chosen to defend our sacred lands."

"Okay then. First thing in the morning, we will pack our gear and plan to head back down the mountain and scout out that outlaw camp again. Let's hit the mats and get some shut-eye, boys," said Nevada.

Chapter VI

THE ESCAPE

Morning arrived fast, and the boys gathered their gear, packing it up for the trip down the mountains. Breakfast was ready, having been prepared earlier by the women of the village. The young buck Indians were already finishing up their meal when Nevada, Cappie, and Smokey stopped by the venison stew pot to get a plate of food. They greeted Keytoe, and Nevada noticed about ten or eleven young Indians already putting on their quivers and checking the feathers on their arrows and the strings of their bows. The young bucks were just about ready to move out. Some of them even donned war paint. *These Indians don't waste any time*, thought Nevada. He felt a kind of excitement building up inside his body, the kind of excitement his Cherokee grandfather must have felt before a big-game hunt.

The group of scouts stealthily descended the mountain following Keytoe, with the three American men bringing up the rear of the group. They traveled over layers of rock, each displaying a different color in the morning sunshine—shales that were red, limestones the color of yellow gray, sandstones in hues of white and brown, and pinkish granite—the colors varying as in the colors of a kaleidoscope. As the sun slanted in a different way, the colors would change again, as if they were moving in a special kind of rhythm across the whispering mountain ridges.

Not a sound could be heard coming from the descent of the Indians with the exception of the faint whisper of their arrows moving back and forth in the quivers. The bucks moved skillfully over the rocks in an indescribable whisper of their soft leather moccasins. Their movement was soundless and mute to human ears. When they reached the soft trickling sound of the rushing brook and waterfall in the rocks, they stopped to rest, drink, and refill their waterskins with fresh water. The steady trickling of the stream over the rocks was the only sound that could be heard. A jackrabbit scurried under a bush across from the stream. The mountain wildlife seemed to know the Indians were there but paid no attention to them since they were a part of the mountain's landscape. Again Nevada noticed the minnows and crayfish living in the clear mountain stream, just as they did on his way up the mountain with Keytoe. The fish paid no heed to what was going on around them. These fish were living in their own silent, free little world, untouched by human invasion. This stream was probably fed by the constant melting of mountain snow. *Mother Nature's silent whispering continues on*, thought Nevada.

Keytoe came over to the three Americans and quietly spoke. "We will proceed to the secret mine where we rested coming up the mountain. I will send out a couple of scouts to check the outlaws' camp and report back to us. We shall wait there until we get a report back from the scouts."

"Okay, Keytoe," said Nevada.

It was not long after that when they reached the cave of the secret mine. They all settled down just inside the entrance of the mine and pulled out dried provisions for a quiet lunch. Keytoe gave orders in his Indian tongue, and three braves disappeared down the mountain rocks in total silence. Nevada shook his head in awe at the skills these young Indians possessed.

It was about two hours later when the three braves appeared back at the mine and reported to Keytoe in their native tongue. They sat down and quickly ate their lunch. Keytoe walked over to the three Americans.

"Nevada, there are three guards. One at the entrance to the camp and one in the rocks on each side of the camp. There are about twelve outlaws left in the camp. The horses are in the corral, unsaddled. If you take back your horses, it will take time to saddle them unless you ride them bareback and leave your saddles behind."

"Those saddles are expensive. I don't want to leave them behind if I can help it," said Nevada.

Smokey and Cappie just looked at each other with a sigh.

"Okay," said Keytoe. "There is no one in the mine shaft as a hostage. They have not captured anyone else. However, there are four outlaws combing the trail for you three Americans. They know you are not on horseback and, therefore, are looking for you down the mountainside to see how far down you may have escaped from them. They are also aware that you were helped by Indians, and they are also looking for us. They must have found one of my arrows."

"Well, now that is not good, Keytoe. I'm sorry I got you mixed up in this mess," said Nevada.

"These outlaws were trespassing on our lands and were our problem to begin with. We shall have to deal with them. You have given us an advantage, my friends, by getting us rifles and showing us how to load and use them. I have a plan all figured out."

Nevada showed great respect for Keytoe's judgment and was willing to cooperate with any plan Keytoe offered. Keytoe was very skilled in his home mountain terrain, and Nevada was ready to go along with anything Keytoe wanted. No wonder he was considered chief and leader of what was left of his tribe. He was a brilliant and skilled boy for his age. Having a mountain man for a father was an added asset to his skills.

They slipped down the mountainside, leaving the shelter of the secret mine shaft behind, and positioned themselves all around the outlaw camp, hiding in the rocks out of site. Keytoe shot an arrow into a tree as a signal, and three scouts slipped up on the three camp guards, stabbing them quietly with their knives. Keytoe shot another arrow into a fallen log near Nevada and Patto, his blood brother. Nevada and Patto slipped down into the corral, and Nevada pointed out the three horses that were their mounts. Patto went after the horses, gathering them together and bringing them over near the side of the corral. At the same time, Nevada gathered the three saddles and set them together near the three horses. Patto stood guard while Nevada saddled the three horses. Patto shot an arrow into a tree, signaling Keytoe that the horses were saddled and ready.

Keytoe gave the signal to attack the camp using rifle fire and bows and arrows. The surprise attack gave the Indians the advantage. Patto opened the corral gate and stampeded the outlaws' horses out of the gate and down the mountainside. Nevada was holding on to their three horses so they wouldn't scatter with the rest of the herd. He tied them tight to the corral fence and, joining the fight, took up his rifle and started shooting the outlaws. Smokey and Cappie were shooting their rifles also. In a matter of twenty minutes, the camp was quiet, and the outlaws were all defeated. The group of Indians and the three Americans met in the middle of the camp. They were shaking hands with each other for a job well done. Nevada, Smokey, and Cappie mounted their horses, reloaded their firearms, and headed down the mountainside in a walk to maybe meet up with the four outlaws that were searching the trail for them. Keytoe's tribe was cleaning up the sacred Indian grounds. They took all the leftover firearms and ammo for themselves and threw the dead bodies in the mine shaft, covering it over with dirt and debris to keep the animals away. They waved good-bye to the three Americans and headed back up the mountain to their secret village home.

CHAPTER VII

HARSHAW

Nevada, Smokey, and Cappie took their time riding the trail down the mountain. They wanted to be sure Pedro and the other three outlaws were not hiding in ambush for them. As they traveled down through the dusty rocky trail, they listened hard for horses with riders coming up the same trail. Their luck was holding out because no one was coming up the trail. The empty trail ended just outside of the town of Harshaw. They would have to carefully slip into town unnoticed. Nevada led them around through the back side of the buildings to the back door of the sheriff's office, where they tethered their mounts behind the building at a hitch rail. Nevada slipped in the front door after unlocking it with the key from his pocket then went inside and unlocked the back door to let in Smokey and Cappie. To Nevada's surprise, their personal belongings were still there where they left them on the bunk when the outlaws escorted them out with their hands tied. They gathered their belongings and packed their horses.

They now needed a plan to take out Pedro and the other three Mexican bandits. The town needed to be searched to find out where these four ended up. They were to secretly search the town and meet up behind the sheriff's office again to devise a plan. When they met up again, they discussed the plan. Two bandits were in the saloon, one was at the livery stable, and Pedro was in Carmelita's apartment.

In order to free the town from the control of the outlaw gang, the bandits had to be overcome. It would also free the sacred Indian grounds from the bandits and Pedro, the leader. The three friends knew they had to finish the job. It was not an option to leave it undone, especially since they owed a debt to the small Indian village for saving their lives.

They took the livery stable first, because it would be the easiest encounter. Smokey covered the front door of the livery while Cappie covered the backdoor escape route. Nevada slipped into the stable to confront the Mexican outlaw. He found the outlaw tending to the horses of the four outlaws. He slipped silently up behind the outlaw and buffaloed him with his gun, knocking the outlaw out cold. Grabbing some rope from a wall peg in the barn, Nevada removed the weapons from the outlaw and tied him up. Smokey and Cappie came in and hustled the man out the back door, dragging him down the back alley behind the buildings, and threw him on a bunk in a jail cell, locking him in. Then the three slipped quietly over to the saloon. The two bandits in the saloon were playing a game of cards at a table and had a bottle of ninety-proof tequila and a couple of glasses that they consistently filled as fast as they emptied them out.

Smokey climbed up the porch to the balcony of the saloon and slipped in through a hall window, taking a position inside the building, at the top of the stairs. Cappie slipped in the back door through the kitchen, taking a position inside the kitchen door where he could see the whole room.

Nevada walked into the saloon through the batwing doors and stood facing the two bandits with his feet apart. When they saw their escaped prisoner standing there as a threat, they drew their guns fast—but not fast enough. The bigger man shot first, missing Nevada, and Smokey took him down from upstairs on the top step, killing the man. Nevada's fast draw significantly beat the other outlaw, sending him to the hereafter. The noise of the gunplay alerted Pedro to trouble, and he dressed and holstered up, running outside the brothel to the street. Nevada walked out the batwing doors and went out to the street, taking a stand in the middle of the road, facing Pedro.

"Oh, gringo. I see it is you again causing trouble for me, eh? I wondered where you got to when you escaped the mine shaft. We looked for you all over the trail. Tell me, how did you get out?" Pedro looked around, trying to find where the members of gang were holed up. When he did not see any of them, he began to get nervous.

"You'll have to find out for yourself how I got out, because I ain't telling you, Pedro," said Nevada. "I don't like being starved half to death down in an abandoned mine shaft."

"Oh, I see you did not like the accommodations, gringo." Pedro laughed. "You did do a lot of complaining while you were down there. You have a very short temper, senor. Maybe next time I can do better for you, gringo. A banquet table with a white table cloth, or perhaps a nice bed with silk covers?"

"There won't be a next time, Pedro. It's adios. As of now, you are finished," replied Nevada.

"We shall see about that gringo." Pedro drew fast, but Nevada cut him down with one shot, finishing him off. The people of Harshaw came running out into the street to see the dead outlaw. They couldn't believe it. These three men cleaned up the town and saved the people from the heckling of a very bad gang of outlaws.

The people of Harshaw were so excited they decided it was time for a fiesta. Everyone was invited to the party in honor of the three Americans who saved the town. Nevada sang the ballad "Thinking of You" at the party. He realized for the first time how much he missed his wife, Ricki, and the obligation he felt to the vow he took on their wedding day. He felt lonely for her company and was anxious to get back home and protect the bond they now had with each other.

The fiesta continued all through the night, with much music and dancing and plenty of good Mexican food. Nevada had a tough time turning away several free offers from dancing, high-spirited senoritas. Smokey had latched onto Carmelita, who he really preferred to all the rest. Rosita brought Nevada a large piece of warm, fresh-baked apple pie, which, to her delight, he wolfed down. Cappie made it pretty plain that Rosita was his girl and stuck to her like glue. Nevada took notice and giggled because he figured as much from the way she talked about him when she first came into the sheriff's office. He knew there was a bond between them of some kind even before he ventured up that mountain to find Cappie.

Nevada was getting tired as the celebration continued on throughout the night, so he told Smokey and Cappie he was turning in for the night and headed back to the sheriff's office to get some much-needed sleep. About an hour later, Smokey staggered in and climbed into the upper bunk. They slept until almost noon the next day and woke up really hungry for something to eat. It was about that same time when Cappie and Rosita came into the office from her casa, with plates of tortillas with salsa and eggs. Boy, what a welcome sight that was! They all ate a hearty breakfast and began to pack their horses for the trip back to Cappie's mountain home. Only this time, Rosita would be going back with them to take care of Cappie's broken arm. Nevada saw the writing on the wall. *I knew this was more of a relationship than a friendship,* he thought. He helped Rosita pack her mount with several of her personal belongings. *Why do women have so much stuff to bring with them?* he thought. *This will slow us down on the trail back up the mountain. She really needs to leave behind half this stuff! Damn. No way am I gonna argue with a woman.*

They left right after lunch, with Nevada leading the way and Smokey taking up the rear to make sure nothing fell off the pack horses and make sure Cappie was okay riding with one arm in a sling. The trail was narrow and rocky. A slight drizzle was coming down. Nevada hoped it would not make the trail muddy and slippery. Six hours of travel and seven o'clock at night put them halfway back to Cappie's mountain home. They stopped to make a night camp to give the horses and Rosita a break from the uphill climb. Nevada was able to hunt down a few good-size rabbits and a couple of mourning doves, and Rosita had hot salsa in her pack to cook them in; stewed rabbit with the doves was a great evening meal for them.

A coyote sang out in the distant hills. Nevada exchanged glances with Smokey and said, "Not again, I hope."

Smokey laughed and said, "He's far away in the mountains, but we will set up a camp guard anyway tonight. You and I will take turns."

The night camp remained quiet, and morning filtered in fast through the pine and oak tree branches, flickering daylight across the pathway. They broke camp after a quick breakfast and headed on up the trail, continuing the journey back to Cappie's home. It was around four o'clock in the afternoon when they reached the house. Since they didn't stop for lunch, they were all starving. Jonah was just finishing up feeding the pack mules and horses and cleaning out the stable when he turned and saw them arriving.

"Welcome back, boys. You found Cappie! Great! Hi, Rosita. Nice to see you back here again. Looks like Cappie will need your help. This is great," replied Jonah.

Nice to see you back here, Rosita? thought Nevada. *Cappie had a lot more going on at his mountain home than he was willing to talk about.* Nevada giggled to himself. *Next time me and Smokey will have to remember not to just barge in on Cappie without giving him a warning.* He looked over at Smokey with a smirk and noticed Smokey had picked up on the comment also, because Smokey silently grinned back at Nevada with that look on his face. As long as he'd known Cappie, he'd never heard Cappie mention anything about any women in his life. He actually thought that Cappie was not interested. Nevada thought Cappie liked being a free spirit. One never knows everything about a man, even when he is a close friend. Their pack mules and personal stuff got unpacked and brought in the house, and the animals were taken care of while Rosita and Jonah prepared an evening meal for all of them. Nevada was a happy fellow because he was given a glass of moonshine for sipping after the meal. Smokey turned to Nevada and said, "Don't think you are off the hook on drying out rules because that's all you are getting. You earned this one drink!" Nevada just looked at Smokey and giggled then said, "We shall see, pard."

"What time are you boys leaving in the morning?" asked Cappie.

"Just as soon as we are packed and ready," replied Nevada. "We have been gone about ten days now, and we were only planning on being away seven. By the time we get back home, it will be almost two weeks. Ricki is likely to send out a search party for me or show up herself." Everyone giggled at the thought of Ricki showing up.

She is spunky enough to do it, thought Smokey. *She holds a tight rein on the Nevada Kid. There is not much of anything he can get away with without her eventually finding out about it.*

CHAPTER VIII

THE JOURNEY HOME

The morning came around fast, and the boys were packing their gear to head on back down the mountains to the Flying T2 Ranch. Nevada felt like this trip put him almost a week behind at the ranch. He would have to work hard to make up for the lost time. The spring calving season was coming into full swing, and he needed to be back there, supervising the roundup and the birthing of the calves. He knew he had capable ranch hands and a good, capable wife running the show. However, he felt he needed and wanted to be there. Without hesitation, they said their good-byes and were heading back on their way home.

The trip down the stony, rubbly mountain would be easier than the trip they did coming up. It would be less than a two-day trip since it was quicker going down. They were careful with the horses in some of the rough places along the trail surface where mud and sand caused unsteady footing. Some of the trail surfaces were loose and rough, but they found them passable. The day was heating up to seventy-five degrees. Purple violets with yellow centers started showing up along the trail, as well as colorful Status sprouting out in the sunny spots as springtime reared its head, showing off the bright greens of fresh new growth. Winter was definitely on its way out as the new season emerged. As they reached the foot of the mountains, fresh meadows of tall, waving grass opened up to small hills and valleys. A herd of wild horses took off, running away from them, manes flying in the spring breezes when the cowboys' unexpected approach startled the herd. The herd, in turn, startled some wild turkeys, which took wing straight across the front of the two riders, who grabbed their rifles and shot one each. At least they weren't going home empty-handed. They bagged two sizable toms, tying their feet and the bag to their saddle horns with piggin' strings. They would dress them out when they got home. Now they were crossing Nevada's rangeland, heading across the property toward the farmhouse, which they could see a mile off in the distance. Ricki saw them walking their horses toward the house when they were about a half mile away. She stood up from her rocking chair and put down her knitting and watched, awaiting their approach. She called to them when they were less than a few yards away. Their horses were breathing heavy.

"Thomas Lacey! Where have you been? You were supposed to be home a week ago!" yelled Ricki from the porch of the farmhouse.

"Uh-oh. Your formal name," whispered Smokey. "She's all yours now, pard."

"You deserting me?" said Nevada under his breath.

"Damn right," replied Smokey. "I'll be at the bunkhouse." He giggled.

"Shit. That ain't fair," whispered Nevada.

"The hell it ain't," replied Smokey. "Hi, Ricki!" He took the turkey from Nevada's horse, dismounted and led the two horses and Lazy Daisy over to the corral. He handed the two turkeys toward Sandy Saunders, who immediately ran up to Smokey taking the turkeys to dress, clean, and pluck them.

"What happened to you two boys? We were getting worried. Thought maybe you were shanghaied," said Sandy. "Ricki was gonna send out a search party."

"I guess you could call it that," replied Smokey. "Cappie was kidnapped, and we went to rescue him and got kidnapped ourselves by the same group of Mexican outlaws. Long story. I'll tell you all about it later tonight in the bunkhouse." Smokey and Sandy started unpacking Jawbone, Lazy Daisy and Tacco.

"Boy, did Ricki get real upset. She was worried about Nevada. Thought somebody with a faster gun done him in. That gal was scared," said Sandy.

"She had good reason to be," replied Smokey. "She was pretty upset with him when we rode up to the porch. Nevada will have to smooth it over with her. Don't tell her, but we came very close to being done in. Cappie's arm got broken, and Nevada was pissed off worse than I've ever seen him. We were stuck in a half-dug-out mine shaft with no way to get out. Nevada's good at taking care of us, but even he plumb ran out of ideas!"

"Geez, Smokey. I'm guessing you didn't get any hunting in," said Sandy.

"Them turkeys is all the hunting we got in. Except we got a wild coyote that almost pounced on Nevada at night camp. Gave the fur to Cappie."

"Sounds like you boys had a pretty rough trip."

"That's putting it very mildly, Sandy. I don't think Nevada is planning on any more hunting trips for long time. On the way home, he mentioned that Cappie can keep his wild, lush ponderosa forest in the high mountain country." Smokey giggled.

Nevada was no sooner off Tacco and handing his reins to Smokey, when Ricki ran into his arms and kissed him, almost forgetting how angry she was with him.

"What is this, darlin'? First you are yelling at me, then you are kissing me and crying. Are you mad at me, or are you happy to see me?" said Nevada.

"Both," cried Ricki.

"Both at the same time? Boy, I've yet to figure you women out." He wiped away her tears with his thumb.

"Just where the hell were you?" she said.

"Well, we had some trouble. Cappie was kidnapped, and he was not home when we got to his place. We had to find him and rescue him. Never got any hunting done."

"Geez, Nevada. Why is your life always so complicated? Nothing ever goes smooth for you or according to your plans."

"Good question, Ricki. If I could change my bad luck, I would." He pulled her in tight against his chest, kissing her passionately. "Boy, did I miss you, darlin'." He could feel his body going rock hard with his need for her. "We got a lot of business to take care of, because I'm in a bad way, and it ain't no joke. Two weeks without you is more than I can take. No more hunting trips for a while, unless I take you with me. I'm really getting into this being married with all its entitlements. I should have done it sooner. Let's go inside the house where there is more privacy, and you can welcome home the boss man properly. Hopefully, none of the ranch hands will disturb us for a while."

She lay in his arms for more than an hour as he slept off the drowsiness that always came after he completely satisfied his male cravings. Ricki suddenly remembered the letter that came for him. Should she wake him from his lethargy or not?

"Nevada," she gently whispered.

"Mmmm," he answered.

"I forgot to tell you about the letter you received from the attorney."

"Huh? What letter?"

"You got a summons to appear in court for the custody trial of TJ. Your Attorney, Mr. Parks, has set the whole thing up for Monday next week," explained Ricki. "Your attorney has you suing John O'Connor for the paternal guardianship rights of your son, Thomas Junior, and Mr. Parks also put in the paperwork to have TJ's last name changed to yours."

"Where's that letter?"

"It's on the table in the kitchen. He gave it to me last week when he saw me in town getting supplies. John O'Connor also got a letter to appear. Mr. Parks told me so when he gave me your letter."

"Wow! That came up in a hurry. I wasn't expecting it so soon. I told him to hold off on the lawsuit for a little while."

"Hold off! It's been more than three weeks since you told him that. Remember, you have been gone for two weeks."

"You're right, Ricki. I somehow lost two weeks out of my life and lost track of where I'm at. I'll read the letter and give him an answer right away tomorrow."

Chapter IX

A CUSTODY BATTLE

"Hear ye, hear ye! The court will come to order. The Honorable John G. Joseph, presiding."

The judge walked in and took the bench. "You may be seated everyone. For the court's record, I would like to explain to you folks that this is a child custody case, and a jury is not needed and will not be present in the courtroom for this case. The case will be presented to the judge—that's me—and I will decide the verdict. However, the plaintiff and the defendant may have attorneys representing them. Also, the plaintiff has said he has no problem with the general public sitting in on the case as witnesses if they so wish. I will remind you that anyone sitting in on the case must hold their tongue or be in contempt of court, and I may remove them at my discretion. Okay, now that that is understood, we shall begin.

"Will the two attorneys please come forward to the bench and introduce themselves to the court. Good morning, gentlemen."

"Good morning, Your Honor. My name is Michael St. John. I'm the attorney for the defendant, John O'Connor, great-uncle of the boy Thomas Trainor."

"Good morning, Your Honor. My name is Stephen A. Parks. I represent the plaintiff, Thomas Lacey, also known as the Nevada Kid, biological father of the boy Thomas Trainor."

"Will the defendant please present to me the summons he received to appear in court, and the plaintiff bring up the letter he received in answer to the summons to appear in court with the court date on it? Thank you, gentlemen. I just need a minute to read them." The judge read the paperwork.

"Okay," said Judge Joseph. "The defendant's attorney may bring up his first witness."

"Your Honor, I call John O'Connor, the defendant, to the stand. Put your hand on the Bible. State your name."

"John O'Connor, sir."

"Do you swear to tell the truth and nothing but the truth in answer to all the questions asked of you, so help you God?"

"Yes, I do."

"Okay, you may take the seat in the witness stand."

"Mr. O'Connor, when was the very first time you met the outlaw Thomas Lacey, also known as the Nevada Kid?"

"Objection, Your Honor. Thomas Lacey is not an outlaw. He did his time and is no longer considered an outlaw wanted by the law. Therefore, he should no longer be referred to as an outlaw or wanted by the law, or a fugitive or any other reference stating that he is outside the law," said attorney Stephen Parks.

"Okay, I agree with you, Mr. Parks. Mr. St. John, you will refrain from referring to the plaintiff in any manner as being against the law, since he paid his dues to society. You may start the questioning over."

"Yes, Your Honor. So, Mr. O'Connor, when was it you first met the *Nevada Kid?*"

"I first met him when he and Smokey came riding up to our front porch. He was shot in the left thigh and was failing fast. Their horses were sweaty and spent, and they were looking for a doctor to help the kid out. My wife, Martha, and I helped the man out because he fell off his horse, almost going unconscious, as we were talking with Smokey. It was like he partially passed out."

"So you had no idea the Nevada Kid was running from the law, took a bullet in the thigh from the posse that was chasing him for breaking a murderer out of jail?"

"No, sir, Mr. St. John," said John O'Connor.

"Your Honor, I object," said Stephen Parks. "Smokey was arrested on *suspicion* of murder only. He was later cleared when the case was solved, and he was found to be innocent. Mr. St. John should not be referring to Smokey as a murderer. Also, Smokey's case is not relevant to this custody case."

"Mr. St. John, you will no longer refer to the Chloride murder case as part of this custody case, and you will no longer refer to Smokey as a murderer. Continue on."

"Yes, sir, Your Honor," said Michael St. John. "So you had no idea these boys were running from the law. You were lied to and told they were ambushed on the trail, they needed a doctor's help, and they needed jobs. So you took the injured young man into your home, gave him a room, and sent to town for the doctor. Is that correct?"

"Yes, sir."

"Did you also pay for the doctor's services on the injured man?"

"Yes, sir. But Tom paid me back out of his wages as soon as he was able to work on the payroll for me."

"So you got him doctored for a week, gave him an honest job, paid him wages for working for you. Buck, your foreman, taught the young man how to be a worthy ranch hand, because as I understand it, the Nevada Kid was a farm boy and knew nothing about ranching. The kid had a free, independent spirit, a short temper, and the only thing he knew was how to be a fast gunman."

"That's right, Mr. St. John," replied John O'Connor.

"So he was now a hired hand working full-time for you. Now tell us what happened in the barn that night. Did he get caught molesting your niece, Polly?"

"I object, Your Honor," said Stephen Parks. "That is a false statement. Tom Lacey did not in any way molest John's niece in the barn. Tell the truth, John."

"Objection overruled. Answer the question, Mr. O'Connor, by what you know that Polly said had happened."

"Polly was preparing to ride out into a very bad thunderstorm to search for a missing student of hers. Tom Lacey saw Polly mounting her horse, Glitter, when he entered the stable to clean the stalls. She said Tom was trying to stop her from riding out into a bad storm that was already upon us, and she was fighting against his stopping her from doing that. Buck, my foreman, walked in on them and thought Tom was trying to have his way with Polly, and Buck's hollering at Tom scared Polly, causing her to lose her balance and fall off Glitter right on top of Tom, making the situation look even worse to Buck. Buck overreacted and beat the kid up very badly, almost killing Tom with his rage. Two of my cowhands were holding Tom's arms back so he couldn't fight back, and Tom was defenseless during the beating because he had lost his gun when Polly accidently kicked it out of his holster and into the next stall."

"So what happened next? You had to call the doctor again. The kid was out of work for a week while still on your payroll, and you picked up the doctor's tab again for the Nevada Kid? Am I right?" said Attorney St. John.

"Yes, I picked up the tab and didn't dock his pay because it wasn't Tom's fault. He was trying to save my niece Polly from going out in a very dangerous storm situation, and Buck overreacted and beat the kid up and used a bullwhip on him for no reason. Tom didn't deserve what he got that time around, because he saved Polly from what would have been a very dangerous mission."

"But what happened next was careless, irresponsible lust and negligence on the part of the Nevada Kid. You want to tell the judge the rest of the story?" said John's attorney.

"Yes, sir. Polly felt sorry for Tom getting so hurt on account of her, so she went to the bunkhouse to visit him and apologize to him for all that had happened," said John O'Connor. "She did this on her own without my knowledge."

"Tell the judge what the Nevada Kid did to her."

"I can't," said John.

"He raped her in his bunk and got her pregnant. Isn't that what he did?" said Attorney St. John.

"Your Honor, I object to that false statement. It was mutual consent, not rape," hollered Attorney Stephen Parks.

"Order in the court! Overruled," said Judge Joseph. "You'll get your turn, Mr. Parks."

"I don't know for sure what exactly happened. No one was there but the two of them," said John O'Connor.

"No more questions for now, Your Honor. Go back to your seat, John. Your Honor, I'd like to call Tom Lacey, the *Nevada Kid*, ex-outlaw and gunfighter, to the stand."

"That last reference was not necessary, Mr. St. John," said the judge. "Nevada, come up here and put your hand on the Bible, son."

Nevada hesitated. He felt like he was going to shoot the cat. His stomach was churning. He wanted to punch John's attorney in the mouth and flatten him right there where he stood. Ricki reached over and gave his hand a squeeze to help Nevada control the fightin' tallow in his craw. It was enough to give him the calming strength to stand up and walk up to the judge. He put his hand on the Bible. His hand felt sweaty and clammy.

"Do you swear to tell the truth, the whole truth, and nothing but the truth, so help you God?" said the judge.

"Yes, sir, I do."

"Sit down in the witness chair, Nevada. I have a question to ask first before you continue, Mr. St. John. Nevada, the incident in the bunkhouse, was it mutual consent?" asked the judge.

"Yes, sir. Absolutely, sir."

"Is there any way you can prove that to me?" said the judge.

"No, sir. Not really, sir."

"Then tell us what happened in the bunkhouse that day."

"We were all alone. I kept telling Polly she didn't belong in the men's quarters. She kept insisting she wanted to stay and wouldn't leave. I told her she had to leave. I had no clothes on under the blankets. She brought a chair over and sat down next to me by the bunk anyway. She told me she loved me, and she bent over and kissed me on my bruised, swollen lip. Her advances toward me aroused me to where I was losing control. What did you expect me to do? I was a man with no clothes on getting kissed by this beautiful girl that I thought I was in love with. She was arousing me, and I guess I just lost it from there. When it was over, she thanked me for loving her. No girl ever said that to me before. I figured she was going to be my girl after that."

"He's lying, Judge," said Attorney St. John. "He's trying to save his own skin and make it look like it all was her idea."

"That's not true. I took an oath on the Bible. I wouldn't lie after taking an oath," said Nevada. His dander was up now, and his vinegar was beginning to show. *This bastard attorney needs a good hard right fist to his jaw to straighten him out*, thought Nevada.

"Take it easy, son. I believe you," said the judge. "Ladies and gentlemen, I am calling for a five-minute break. I would like to have the attorneys come up to the bench. The rest of you leave the room for five minutes, and then you can come back. Thank you."

The spectators went outside on the boardwalk, emptying out the courtroom. The two attorneys went up to the judge. "I have a very personal question to ask this young man and want no one to hear it but you two attorneys. Nevada, did you know at the time you made love to Polly that there was good chance she was impregnated with your seed?"

"I was afraid that was what you would ask me, Judge," said Nevada. He let out a sigh. He put his hands over his face and tensed up really tight, taking in a deep breath and letting it out. "I thought this was a simple custody case. I didn't know the questions would be so personal and so hard to answer."

"Well? I'm waiting for the answer," said the judge.

"Yes, sir. I knew immediately. I lost my concentration, and it all went downhill from there. It was then I planned on marrying her just as soon as I got back from the cattle drive. There was no question in my mind. I intended to marry her because I believed I loved her and the feeling was mutual."

"You planned on marrying her even before you knew for sure she was pregnant?"

"Yes, sir, Your Honor."

"Even if she wasn't pregnant when you got back from the cattle drive, were you still planning on marrying her?"

"Yes, sir, that was my intention."

"Okay, son," said Judge Joseph. "That answers my question and tells me a lot about you and the fact that you were raised with good morals. Attorney Parks, it's your turn, and you may call your first witness to the stand as soon as the people file back in here and take their seats. Mr. St. John, you may sit down. Nevada, you may go back to your seat—unless, of course, you are the next first witness."

The people filed back into the courtroom and sat down now that the break was over with.

"I wonder what they were talking about while we were outside for the break," whispered Cappie to Smokey.

"No question in my mind what the judge asked by the upset look on Nevada's face. It was a damned embarrassing personal question. Nevada is clearly stressed. I talked to the kid like a father right after that incident, and he had the same look on his face then." Nevada looked directly at Smokey and then looked down at the floor, feeling embarrassed.

The gavel slammed down a couple of times. "Order in the court! The next session of this court will now begin," replied Judge Joseph. "The attorney for the plaintiff will now come forward and call his first witness to the stand."

"Your Honor, I would like to have Nevada as my first witness."

"Okay, Mr. Parks. Nevada, stay on the witness stand because you are still under oath. You may proceed, Mr. Parks. No, wait a minute. *Okay*, who brought the boy Thomas Trainor in here after the break? Please remove the young boy from my court until I call for him to be brought in here. There is some questioning going on here that I do not want the boy to hear. His time to come into this court will be when I invite him to be brought in and no sooner. There will be no child brought into this hearing that is under the age of twenty-one."

Nevada stood up, showing his irritation.

"I'm sorry, Your Honor. I brought him in here, so I'll take him outside," said one of John O'Connor's cowhands. He took TJ's hand and walked him outside.

"Okay, Mr. Parks. You may proceed as soon as the boy leaves the building. Stay in the witness chair, Nevada, and sit down."

"Judge, I'm calling Mr. Tom Lacey as my first witness. Your Honor, I would like to make a few statements before I start my questioning."

"Proceed, Mr. Parks."

"Mr. St. John stated that Mr. Lacey was trying to save his own skin by making it look like the romantic interlude in the bunkhouse was all the girl Polly's fault. *Well, I ask you, Judge, and I ask the general public, what girl walks into a bunkhouse, the men's quarters, without knocking, and walks right up to a cowboy who's in his bunk with no clothes on under his blankets, pulls up a chair, sits down, and proceeds to kiss him on his bruises and then expects that nothing is going to happen?*"

The courtroom was in a fitful roar. "Order in the court!" said the judge, slamming down the gavel several times. "Order in the court! Mr. Parks, your statement has been noted by everyone in this room, so may I recommend you hold down your personal opinions during questioning so as not to cause any riots in my court? If you can do so, then let's continue with this case. Do not address the audience. You are to address me only."

"Yes, Your Honor. Mr. Lacey, did Polly knock before coming into the bunkhouse to see you?"

"No, sir, she didn't."

"When did you first know she was there?"

"I, uh, guess it was when she walked up next to the bunk, and I caught her movement. I was reading a magazine. I ditched it fast under the covers when I saw her so I wouldn't offend a lady with off-color reading material."

Laughter resounded throughout the courtroom. "Order. Order," said the judge.

"So what did you say to her when you saw her, Mr. Lacey?"

"I said 'Jeez, Polly, what are you doing in here?' and I pulled the blanket up to the top of my chest to cover up my nakedness."

"Then what happened?"

"Well, she laughed at me as if to say 'I saw what you were reading.' Then she said, 'I came to see how you are feeling.'"

"What did you say to that, Mr. Lacey?" asked Mr. Parks.

"I said, 'Get out of here now. This building is off-limits to women.'"

"Your Honor, ladies and gentlemen of the audience, Mr. Lacey said 'Get out of here now. This building is off-limits to women.' *I ask you now, does that sound like an invitation to the young lady to join him for sex in the bunkhouse?*"

"No" was murmured throughout the audience. "No."

"Order in the court," repeated the judge.

"I object to this kind of dialogue, Your Honor," yelled Attorney St. John. "This is not an audience-participation trial hearing."

"You are right, Mr. St. John. Mr. Parks, I must advise you again not to address the audience with your questions. If you can follow that rule, you may proceed."

"Okay, Your Honor. Mr. Lacey, what did Polly say when you told her the bunkhouse was off-limits to women?"

"She said, 'But I wanted to see you and tell you how sorry I am that I ran away like a coward. I didn't mean to get you in trouble at the stable. I ran and got Uncle John as fast as I could to stop the fight.' So I told her, 'Get out of here now before someone comes and I get in trouble again. My body can't take another beating like the one I just got.'"

"What did she say to that?" asked Mr. Parks.

"She said, 'I'm very fond of you, and I've fallen in love with you.' Then she kissed me on my swollen, cut lip. I couldn't control myself. My emotions were getting away from me. What do you expect of me, Judge? We had deep feelings for each other. We had fallen in love!"

"Your Honor, let me sum this up quickly here," said Attorney Parks. "This is not a trial on the love affair of Polly and Tom. It is a custody trial on the guardianship of their son. What happened to Tom Lacey and Polly Trainor was unfortunate indeed. But it was not the fault of either one of them. Circumstance caused them to fall in love and have a child out of wedlock. This young man lost his self-control for a beautiful girl, and it can happen to any young man. He carried the burden of the mistake on the cattle drive with him for three months, not knowing if Polly was pregnant or not. He was totally considerate of the young lady and *came back*. Tom could have taken off for parts unknown or even join back up with the Younger Brothers' Gang, *but he didn't. He showed up* after the cattle drive and asked her uncle John for her hand in marriage. And what happened? Her uncle, John O'Conner, would not grant him the permission to marry her. Polly *wanted* to marry Tom Lacey, so actually, whose fault was it that the child did not have both a father and a mother? You can't blame Tom Lacey for that! *It was Mr. John O'Connor's fault*. Then what does Mr. O'Connor do next? Instead of giving his consent for them get married, Mr. O'Connor turns the Nevada Kid in to law enforcement, collects the reward money, and Nevada gets sent to prison for five years. He gets out of prison and works the rodeo circuit. In the meantime, Polly dies of the fever before Tom gets back to her. That, Your Honor, was an act of God, so you can't blame Tom Lacey for Polly's loss either. Hasn't this man been made to suffer enough? Nevada then buys a ranch, becomes a respectable citizen, and now wants to raise his son on his new ranch. So I ask you, Your Honor, what is *wrong* with doing the *right* thing for his son now? Just how much more suffering does this man have to go through to get things right in his life? I have no more questions for this witness, Your Honor."

"Mr. St. John. Do you have any more questions for the witness Thomas Lacey?" said Judge Joseph.

"No, Judge, I don't. Not right at this moment. But I would like to call Mrs. Ricki Lacey to the stand for some questions as a witness, Your Honor."

"Mrs. Lacey, would you please take the stand? Mr. Lacey, you may step down and be seated," replied Judge Joseph.

Tom gave the dirtiest look at Attorney St. John. *What does he want with Ricki? Why drag her into this?* he thought. Nevada's dander was showing again.

"Mrs. Lacey, put your hand on the Bible. Do you swear to tell the truth, the whole truth, and nothing but the truth, so help you God?"

"Yes, Your Honor, I do."

"You may proceed, council," said Judge Joseph.

"Mrs. Lacey, how long have you known the plaintiff before you married him?" said Mr. St. John.

"A year and a half, maybe two years. I met him when he arrived at the Broken Arrow Ranch looking for rodeo work."

"How did he approach you?"

"What do you mean?"

"How did the relationship start?"

"He saved my life and the life of half a dozen barrel racers. Our wagon was out of control and running down the dirt road coming from the ranch. He was watering his horse at the bridge, and it was like he came out of nowhere and got the wagon under control, stopping it and saving our lives. We were very grateful he was there to help us. He had just arrived at the Broken Arrow looking for a job."

"When did you actually start having a personal relationship with him?"

Ricki looked at Nevada as if to say "Do I have to answer all this stuff?" Nevada was getting pissed and fidgeted in the seat showing his discomfort.

"Your Honor," interrupted Attorney Parks when he saw Ricki's puzzled face exchange a glance with Nevada and Nevada's obvious discomfort with the question. "What does Mrs. Lacey's relationship with the plaintiff have to do with a custody case?"

Mr. St. John explained, "Your Honor, I'm trying to establish the fact that the Nevada Kid had an ongoing relationship with this woman at the same time everyone said he had intentions of marrying Miss Polly. If that was the case, Your Honor, then the Nevada Kid had no honorable intentions of marrying Miss Polly. He was leading Miss Polly along falsely while having another relationship going on at the same time at the Broken Arrow Ranch with his present wife. The man is a womanizer!"

"I am not a womanizer!" yelled Nevada. "I never had to chase any woman. They all came to me and hung on me like flies on shit!"

"You got that right, cowboy. You're nothing but shit."

"How dare you talk to him like that?" screamed Ricki.

The judge sighed. "Order in my court! Mr. St. John, I'd like to get this case back to a custody case," said the judge. "I'm not interested in what Mr. Lacey's relationships with other women are, and I'm sure there were many of them while he was out there on the trail being a free spirit." Laughter came from the audience. "Order in the court," reminded the judge. Nevada just shook his head. He didn't like where any of this questioning in the case was going.

"Your Honor, I'm trying to prove here that Mr. Lacey is unfit as a father."

"Well, then prove your case by keeping it to child-raising and not relationships," said the judge.

"Yes, Your Honor. Mrs. Lacey, is it true your husband is a heavy drinker?"

"Well, he was before we got married, but he has reformed. He is very careful about his drinking now. He knows I won't stand for it."

"When exactly did his drinking problem start? Do you know, or was he always heavy into liquor and saloon entertainment?"

"I resent that question to my wife," said Nevada.

"Be quiet, young man. You are not on the stand now. Continue. Answer the question, Mrs. Lacey," said Judge Joseph.

"His drinking problem started when Polly died. He broke up with me to tell me he was going back for Polly and his son. When he heard she died, the pain of her loss was more than he could bear, and he got roostered and tried to kill himself with rotgut whiskey out on the desert. His friends saved him and dried him out. He is doing fine now."

"Your Honor, the Nevada Kid is incapable and unfit of making decisions about TJ's upbringing," said Attorney St. John. "He has an alcoholic background, and he has a past reputation as a womanizer, a former outlaw and gunslinger, and even tried to commit suicide. Does this sound like a stable person? He has no idea of the responsibilities that go along with raising a child."

"That is not true, Your Honor!" said Ricki.

"What can you say on your husband's behalf, Mrs. Lacey, in that he can handle children and be a responsible father?" inquired the judge.

"Well, Your Honor, how much more experience can a man have raising a child than when he is about to be a new father again in September?" said Ricki. "Doesn't that count for something if he is raising another one?"

"What?" shouted Nevada. "What did you just say, Ricki?"

"I'm pregnant," said Ricki to Nevada.

"Shit! Why am I always the last one to find out about my own personal business?"

Laughter exploded in the courtroom. "Order in the court!" yelled the judge. He slammed the gavel down.

"Because you never pay that much attention to what is going on in your personal life. You are too busy ranching," replied Ricki.

"Order in the court," replied Judge Joseph. "Mrs. Lacey, only answer the questions you are asked by the attorneys. Don't be adding to them."

"Sorry, Judge, but I'm not done with him yet. Besides, Nevada, I thought you noticed," said Ricki.

"Well, hell. I noticed that you were putting—"

"Nevada!" hollered out Smokey. Nevada turned his head around and looked back at Smokey with a question on his brow. "Don't finish that sentence, compadre, or you will be sleeping in the bunkhouse with the rest of us for a while."

"Shit," said Nevada.

Laughter exploded again in the courthouse. "I said, order in the court," replied the judge again. "You two continue this argument of yours at home in privacy and not in my courtroom. Nevada, one more bomb of discouraging words from you in my court, and I'm holding you in contempt of court."

"All right, scratch my last remark, Judge," said Nevada. More laughter in the courtroom. Nevada had a sheepish grin on his face and shook his head. "I hope it's a boy."

"With your wild testosterone, why would it be anything else but a boy?" said Cappie.

Laughter exploded again.

"I said, order in my court." The gavel slammed down on the judge's desk. "Order in this courtroom! I'm gonna tell you cowboys just one more time. No more outbursts or harassing of the plaintiff, or I'll throw you all out of my courtroom. I must remind you all that this here is a serious custody trial. Now can we continue on with the hearing?" said Judge Joseph. "Now if Attorney St. John has no more questions for Mrs. Lacey, she may step down, and we will continue on with another witness."

"I have no more questions for her, Your Honor."

Ricki came down from the witness stand and sat next to Nevada. He took her hand and kissed it. They exchanged silent glances.

"Your Honor, I think it's time we bring in young Thomas Trainor for a few questions, sir," said Attorney Parks.

Nevada and Ricki continued to look at each other with concerned expressions.

"I agree with you. Somebody go outside and bring in the boy." Smokey got up immediately and went outside to fetch Tom Junior. Holding Tom Junior's hand, he walked the boy up to the witness stand. Smokey gave the boy's hand a secret squeeze as if telling him something. No one noticed it.

"Now since this young fellow is an underage child, I will ask the questions of him, and the attorneys will just listen," replied Judge Joseph. "Son, hold up your right hand and put your left hand on this Bible. Do you promise to tell the truth, the whole truth, and answer all my questions truthfully, young man?"

"Yes, sir," said TJ.

"State your name and your age, young man," said Judge Joseph.

"Thomas Trainor, sir, and I'm ten years old."

"Do you know why you are in court today, son? If so, please state it."

"Because my pa wants me to live with him on his ranch."

"TJ, do you like your father?"

"Sure. What kid wouldn't like my father? He is the best all-around cowboy I ever knew. He can rope, ride rough stock in the rodeo, and he is a fast gun and can outshoot anybody." Nevada's eyes looked up at the ceiling when the kid said that. He breathed out a quiet sigh. "What kid wouldn't want a father as famous as him? I'm a lucky kid!"

Ricki looked Nevada in the eyes and gave him a stern look. Nevada gave her a look back, showing the palms of his hands, as if to say "What can I tell you?"

"TJ, where do you want to live? With your father or with the O'Connors?"

"I want to live with my father, Judge. I never had a father, and I want to be with my father because he is a real neat guy. I like being with him."

Nevada silently smiled at his boy.

"TJ, you know this means you have to behave yourself and not cause any trouble? You have to go to school and listen to your new mother and father. Do you understand that?" replied Judge Joseph.

"Yes, sir. But I am a boy, sir. Boys are not perfect, you know."

"I know that, young man. I also know that you got your father's blood in you, which means you are a chip off the old block, and it will take a lot more effort on your part. You will have to try much *harder* than most boys to behave." Nevada cringed. Laughter throughout the courtroom. "Order," said the judge, slamming down the gavel. Nevada shifted in his seat, looking up at the ceiling again, sighing.

"Your Honor," interrupted John O'Connor. "Will my wife and I ever get to see the boy again should you award custody to Tom Lacey?"

"Yes," replied the judge. "You may see him as his new parents will allow visiting rights."

"TJ is not a prisoner, Your Honor. He can see the O'Connors anytime he wants to ride over there. No restrictions on my part. After all, they are his great-aunt and great-uncle," said Nevada.

"Now that is very considerate of you, Nevada," said the judge. "This court has made a judgment on this case, and here is what I have determined to be the proper finding: *Nevada has paternity rights to his child. The state of Arizona always awards the child to its one living parent. The great-aunt and great-uncle have not proven preponderance of the evidence, and their argument was not more convincing to me than the argument of the boy's natural father. Unless for any reason the child refuses to live with the parent or the parent is outside the law and unworthy of the child, only then will the state award the custody to the relatives. That is not the case here. TJ said he is willing to live with his father and give it a try. Nevada is a property owner, he has a lucrative stock business, he has a respectable wife, and he is planning to start a new family. He is no longer an outlaw or running from the law. So unless anyone can prove he will not make a good father, come forward with evidence and the direct proof.*"

"Your Honor, this man will surely turn the boy into an outlaw like he once was himself!" yelled John O'Connor. "Can't you see that, Judge? He has no respect for women or the law. He drinks heavily. Where do you see good morals?"

"That is not the case I am trying here, John. Has this man ever shown a history of physical, emotional, or sexual abuse to *children*?" inquired the judge. "That is the case I'm trying, and does anyone have any proof of such a history on this man?"

"No. No proof of that, Your Honor," said Nevada's attorney.

"He is disrespectful with women, Your Honor," said John O'Connor's attorney. "Look what he did to John's niece, Polly? He is a drifter, a no-account, irresponsible cowboy!"

"He is not!" yelled Ricki. "He has been an honorable and respectable husband to me. He is a changed man, a business owner. A good one too, I must say. Maybe Mr. O'Connor should have let him marry Polly, *and we wouldn't be here today*!"

"Ricki!" said Nevada.

"Order in the court!" The gavel slammed down. "Nevada's relationships with women are not relevant to this case. We are talking about the best interests of the child. Nevada is not on trial here for his personal relationships with women. We are talking about parenting and what his relationship will have on the boy as far as parenting goes. I want these suggestive imageries kept down since we have a minor in this courtroom. Furthermore, I will not tolerate any more outbursts in my court from anyone."

"TJ, what do you think of Mr. Thomas Lacey as a father?" asked the judge.

"He is a good father," said TJ. "He taught me how to fish and how to field-dress a fish, and he made sure I got home safely before dark."

"Okay, son, relax. As far as this court is concerned, the boy just said it all," said Judge Joseph. *"This court awards the boy to his natural father, Thomas Lacey, and his lawful wife, Recordina Lacey. It also approves the paperwork that was submitted by Mr. Lacey's attorney, on Mr. Lacey's behalf, to have the boy's last name changed from Trainor, his mother's maiden name, to Lacey, his father's name. I shall sign that paperwork also, because kinship legal guardian is not permitted to consent to the adoption of the child or a name change of the child, as these rights remain with the child's birth parents only. Nevada, you can pick the boy up next Saturday and take him and his belongings to your ranch. Mr. and Mrs. O'Connor will relinquish the boy to the custody of his natural father on Saturday by order of this court.*" The gavel slammed down.

Nevada ran up to the witness stand and took TJ in his arms and hugged him soundly, showing some emotion. TJ hugged his father back. The judge immediately knew he had made the right decision for both the boy and the father. Cheering resounded from all the Flying T2 Ranch hands.

"Order in the court!" said the judge, slamming the gavel down. "We are not done here as yet. There is also a matter of this other counter complaint that has been filed from John O'Connor against Mr. Lacey for the guardian fund."

"What complaint?" replied Nevada. He sat down on the witness chair, holding the boy on his lap.

"Don't you know anything about the guardian fund that the boy's guardian is in charge of, Mr. Lacey?" asked the judge.

"No, sir! What is that? What is this guardian fund?" replied Nevada.

"Let me explain it to you, son. You have been on the cattle trails and ranges for so long you lost touch with the banks and certain legal procedures associated with the court system. When John O'Connor turned you and Smokey in for the reward money on your heads, he took that reward money and put it aside in a guardian fund for the boy's education and upbringing. Whoever has custody of the boy also gets custody of the fund. You had twenty-five hundred dollars on your head, and Smokey had a thousand. There is a guardian fund for thirty-five hundred dollars that goes with the custody of the boy. Since you won custody of the boy, John O'Connor is now suing you for that guardian fund to remain with him, so you won't have power of attorney over your own reward money. The fund was in Polly's name and was transferred to John O'Connor when Polly died and John O'Connor became legal guardian of TJ. Now the fund will go to you since the court awarded you as the new guardian of the boy. Mr. O'Connor is suing you to keep that fund out of your hands."

"No wonder he wouldn't let me have custody of my boy without going to court. I don't care about the money. I just wanted my boy," said Nevada.

"Well, you have to care about the money now because there is now a lawsuit against you for the guardian fund," said the judge. Nevada just shook his head.

"So give him the money, if that's all he wants. If that's the reason why he kept me from marrying Polly and having my son, give him the damn money. I don't want it! I just want to hug my son. The boy means the whole world to me. The money means *effing* nothing to me."

"Watch your cusswords, Nevada. I warned you before about it in this court of law. You are not out on the range. You are in town with decent folk."

"But I didn't say it, I said *effing*!"

"I know what you said, and we all know what you meant. Listen up, Nevada. I figured it out during the trial, Nevada, that you weren't in it for the money," said Judge Joseph. "John, what would you do with the money if I awarded it to you now that you don't have the boy?"

"Probably use it on ranch improvements, Your Honor. What else could I spend it on now? The money came to me for turning in the outlaws anyway, and I gave it to Polly out of the kindness of my heart, for the boy's education. I didn't mean for Nevada to end up with it. You just can't award him his own reward money, Judge. It was mine in the first place for turning those two varmints in."

"Nevada, would you use the reward money on ranch improvements too?"

"Hell no. I'll have two kids to educate now. I'll send them to colleges back East. I'm sure that's what Polly and Ricki would want." Ricki was shaking her head yes.

The gavel came down with a loud slam, startling everyone. *"This court has made a judgment on the guardian fund as well and awards it to Mr. Thomas Lacey and his son, Thomas Junior, for TJ's college education and anything else that Mr. Lacey feels TJ needs. This court is hereby adjourned."*

"No! No, you can't do that," said Mr. O'Connor.

"The trial is closed, Mr. O'Connor," said Judge Joseph.

Cheering resounded throughout the courthouse, and everyone stood up, exiting the building as Judge Joseph signed off on all the paperwork. He handed copies of the paperwork out to both attorneys involved. Some of the wranglers were shaking hands with Nevada and wishing him and Ricki well. Mr. and Mrs. O'Connor were visibly upset as they prepared to leave the courtroom with their attorney and TJ.

"I'm sorry, Mr. and Mrs. O'Connor. I really thought I could win this case against this badass cowboy. I was counting on him hanging himself on his own testimony. It just didn't work out the way I figured it would," said Mr. St. John.

"Well, we can't change what happened, Mr. St. John. He *is* the boy's father, and the state laws were all against us," said John O'Connor.

Nevada walked over to where the O'Connors were standing talking to their attorney.

"TJ, I'll pick you up on Saturday. I'll come over in my ranch supply wagon. You can put all your stuff in there. Okay, TJ?" said Nevada.

"Okay, Pa," said TJ. Nevada gave TJ another big hug, and TJ left with Mr. and Mrs. O'Connor.

CHAPTER X

BACK AT THE RANCH

On Tuesday Nevada was back to the grubby business of no-frills ranching and the unending struggle to survive raising cattle and rough stock for the rodeo circuit, thus pushing forward with his tough will to succeed. Smokey helped him plant some ponderosa pines around the yard as a windbreak, and it gave the ranch an appearance of a prosperous spread. A desert cloudburst gave the pines enough water to start a root system. A couple of snakes slid out of the rocks to enjoy the cool rain, and Nevada did nothing to destroy them since snakes eat the rats that come out of the desert, making them more useful than harmful. Across his rangeland, his cowhands were moving a horse herd to a pasture in the northern upland valley where there was a flowing stream and a corral.

"Smokey, I've got to catch up with Sandy. I need to make an addition on the ranch house before the new baby comes."

"What do you want, Nevada?" inquired Smokey.

"I thought maybe a large master bedroom, and then I could use our bedroom for the nursery. It would give Ricki plenty of room to work with the new baby."

"I'll see him later on this evening and have him draw up some plans for you to look at and approve."

"Sounds good to me," replied Nevada.

"Hey, Nevada, Woolly Bear came down from the south range. He said he needs help pulling cattle from bogholes. They were wandering in there looking for water, or they were just trying to get away from heel flies by wallowing in the deep mud."

"Send Sparky and Che Che Bean to help him out. It shouldn't take more than three of them to get that job done and get the cattle out."

"Okay, boss," replied Smokey. "They are in the northern upland valley moving the rumuda. I'll send them to the south range as soon as they get done."

Wednesday was another busy day on the range. The cattle needed to be worried over and watched continuously. The cowboy life was not a glamorous lifestyle. In fact, it was very boring and monotonous. The herds of cattle had to be doctored for blowflies. It was a dirty job.

"Hey, Smokey," said Nevada. "That old mossy horn has been hooking some young cows in the south pasture. Blowflies are laying eggs in the open wounds and castrations. Get Woolly Bear, Sandy, and Sparky over there to check for screwworms. I got some animals in agonizing pain, and they need to be taken care of right away."

"Okay, Nevada. I'll ride down to the barn and mix carbolic acid and axle grease to put on the skin abrasions."

"Use kerosene if you don't have enough mix to do the job. But if you douse them with kerosene, keep them far away from the branding fires. I don't want any cows turning into living torches and igniting the whole range."

"Gotcha, boss," said Smokey.

Every single day on the range had a boring, monotonous chore that had to be taken care of by the ranch hands.

Thursday approached fast but not with any less responsibilities than what Tuesday and Wednesday brought forth. Smokey and the cowboys had to patrol fifteen to twenty miles of fencing, repairing the parts that washed out in storms. This was a thankless job that had to be done every week.

During droughts in the summertime, the cowhands had to keep a constant watch for fires on the rangeland. Sometimes firebreaks had to be plowed to keep a big range safe.

Friday came roaring in with a desperate job that had to be taken care of immediately. Cattle were lost to predators in the north range. A wolf pack was moving in and stalking the cattle. They had to be found and taken out. The cowboys worked all day tracking down and overtaking the wolf pack using rifles and pistols, riding them down. It was an exhausting chore that caused a very late supper hour and an early bedtime for all of them.

For the first time in ages, Nevada got to sleep late on Saturday morning and got up around eight o'clock instead of four o'clock. Ricki had a very nice breakfast prepared for him, and he took his time eating it and enjoying it. He also took his time cleaning up and shaving this morning because this was the day he was going to get TJ and bring him home at long last. He just couldn't wait to make this happen. It was something he dreamed about for a long time, and his stomach was rolling with both excitement and nervousness.

Nevada went out to the barn to check out the supply wagon and hitch the horses. He met Smokey out there, who was working on cleaning stalls and feeding the horses.

"Hi, compadre. How you doing?"

"Okay, Smokey. I'm really nervous about today," replied Nevada.

"Nothing to it, buddy. It will be a piece of cake. I already fed and brushed down the horses for you. You just need to hitch them up to the wagon."

"Thanks, Smokey."

"If you want, I'll ride over there with you. Facing those O'Connors ain't gonna be an easy chore."

"No, Smokey. This is something I need to do by myself. Thanks anyway, buddy."

"I understand, compadre. I just thought maybe I could help make the trip easier for you."

"Facing the O'Connors will be the hardest thing I'll ever have to do in my life," said Nevada. "The adrenaline will be worse than riding a rank bull like Buck Frenzy for the first time."

"Ain't that the truth," replied Smokey. "Well, you look nice and presentable with your new shirt on."

"Thanks, Smokey. Ricki decided on what I should wear to look my best."

"Hey, Nevada, Sandy has the new addition drawn up for you. You gonna have some time to look at it tonight? He added on two bedrooms instead of one. Said it would be easier to build it that way, with two rooms straight across the back of the house. It would give you a guest room to spread out into, and you will have four bedrooms, instead of just three. How's that?"

"All right. Tell him to come up to the house after supper, and I'll take a look at it." Nevada finished hooking up the team and was getting ready to drive them over to the O'Connor ranch.

Nevada drove the wagon slowly over to the O'Connor ranch. He was taking his time, thinking. He knew what he had to do. His gut was aching. He was avoiding it since the first day he got back to Yuma. There was no avoiding it now; it had to happen. He halted the wagon on the side of the road, jumped down, and picked a bouquet of wildflowers. His gut felt like he was going to shoot the cat. It was something he had to get done and taken care of immediately. There was no turning back. He felt like he wanted to run away and knew he couldn't do that anymore. At this stage in his life, he was beyond running away from himself and his bad luck. It was something that he had to face alone, something that had to be done. No turning back, he was a man now. He found himself driving the team up the long dirt road leading to the O'Connor ranch. Stopping in front of the barn, he got out with the bouquet of flowers in his hand. He reluctantly walked up to the family burial plot in the grove behind the house and immediately found Polly's grave marker. Kneeling down, he placed the bouquet of flowers on her grave. He stayed there a long time. It was painful, but he forced himself to stay there and say a prayer.

Martha was working in the kitchen when she saw someone kneeling on the grave and called to John in the other room.

"Someone is up at Polly's grave," she said to John. John came immediately and looked out the kitchen window with her.

"Why, that's Tom Lacey," said John. "It's about time he paid her some respect."

"Look, John. He put flowers on the grave, and John, he looks like he's crying."

"He is crying, Martha! That young man is so leathery I didn't think he knew how to cry a tear or be tender or sensitive about anything. When Buck nearly beat him to death in the barn, he never shed a tear or showed any emotion but anger."

"I'll go out there are talk to him," said Martha.

"No, Martha. Leave him alone. He's crying because he is alone. He doesn't know we are watching him. Leave him to his private time. Maybe you should go and tell TJ that his father is here. He is upstairs, packing."

"Okay, I will do that," said Martha.

John continued to watch Nevada at the gravesite. Nevada was shaking his head and then bowed it down low toward his knees. *Well, I'll be damned,* thought John. *He did love her. Well, I would never have thought it, the way it all went down. Son-of-a-bitch. That Nevada Kid can feel something. What a surprise to me.*

Nevada stood up and continued to look at the gravesite. He pulled out his neckerchief and wiped his face to get his composure, replacing it in his pocket as he turned around. Then he walked back, going around to the front of the house. As he came up the porch steps, TJ came flying out the door into his father's arms. He hugged his son.

"Pa, I'm all packed. I was so afraid you would change your mind and not come for me," he said.

"Why would I do that?" replied Nevada.

"I don't know. I was just scared you may not want me."

"Don't be silly, boy. We are going fishing tomorrow," said Nevada. "How much stuff you got to put in the wagon? I'll help you carry it all downstairs."

The O'Connors just looked at him in silence, not letting him know what they had just witnessed at the gravesite. Nevada took notice of how very solemn they were acting. Everyone helped load the wagon with TJ's personal belongings. The whole time, Martha was giving instructions to Nevada. "Now you have to remember to tell Ricki that TJ is allergic to molasses but he can have fresh honey. Don't let him get out of the habit of cleaning up his room. He sometimes throws his stuff around and doesn't pick up after himself and needs to be reminded. And he forgets to say *please* and *thank you*."

"Thank you, ma'am. We will be sure to take care of him proper." Nevada smiled at her. She was acting just like he remembered his own mother acting. Women were all alike when it came to kids. "He will be fine, ma'am. You know you are welcome to come over to the ranch anytime you want, ma'am. TJ has no restrictions either. He can visit you anytime he wants to. He just has to let us know when he is going."

"Okay," said Martha. "Next Friday I will bring him his favorite hot apple pie."

"Is that the same hot apple pie you used to make for me when I stayed at the house?"

"Why, yes, it is. I forgot about that, Tom," said Martha.

"We will both be looking forward to that apple pie, ma'am," replied Nevada. "Let's go, cowboy. I got ranch work waiting for me. Say good-bye to Aunt Martha and Uncle John."

"Good-bye. I love you both." He gave them a hug and a kiss.

"Good-bye, TJ," they said. "You listen to your new mom, ya hear?" said Martha.

"Yes, ma'am, Aunt Martha," TJ replied. He tied his red pony to the back of the wagon and climbed in with no trouble.

Nevada noticed the hitch was tied perfectly. *Good boy*, he thought.

Nevada slapped rein, and the wagon took off down the road. It was a great feeling to be taking his boy home. He just didn't know how to put it into words. The boy was his, and he loved him very much. Nobody better ever try and take his kid from him again. There would be hell to pay if they did. He had his family now: a beautiful wife and his son and one more child on the way. Life could not be better than this for him. He also had his dream ranch. There was nothing more in life he could ever wish for or desire. It just didn't get any better than this.

TJ had everything he wanted also. He could not wait to tell all his schoolmates that he was living with his real father now, the Nevada Kid. How exciting this was for a young boy. Just knowing he had a famous father thrilled him. Wow, was he a lucky kid! There would be a lot of stories to tell the other kids. He would become the most popular boy in school.

Nevada pulled up in front of the ranch house. Smokey came over from the corral and helped unload the wagon and bring TJ's belongings into the house, to his new bedroom. Ricki came out on the porch to supervise. All through the house, you could whiff the sourdough biscuits she was baking for supper.

When the wagon was empty, Smokey took it over to the barn to unhitch the horses and put them in the corral. He noticed on the floor of the wagon where Nevada was sitting lay some long-stemmed wildflowers, which he figured fell out of a bouquet. He didn't have to ask. He knew exactly where they came from and what Nevada did with them. He knew Nevada had come full circle and the kid was now a full-grown man. Smokey knew he did not have to be a father image to Nevada any longer. From now on, it was a boss-and-foreman relationship and a good friendship. Perhaps the fathering Smokey did could be transferred to Nevada's son, TJ. He knew for a fact that he and Cappie and all of Nevada's cowhands were going to be looking after the boy's ranching skills, education, and welfare. They all had an interest in this spunky young boy that was a clone of the Nevada Kid.

Smokey went to the back of the wagon and untied TJ's pony and walked it over to the corral. He let it run into the corral with the other horses. *Boy, there was something awful familiar about that pony. If I didn't know any better, I'd say that colt looked like a foal from Nevada's favorite horse, Rusty. Same markings,* he thought. Rusty had died of old age while Nevada and Smokey were in Yuma prison. He remembered how upset Nevada was when he received word in prison about Rusty's loss. Nevada was full of punch and vinegar when he wasn't there to see it all go down. Rusty was being boarded at the O'Connor ranch, and no one said anything about him siring a colt. Smokey decided that he must remember to ask questions about that nice young animal. His suspicions were strong, but there was no proof that it was Rusty's colt. He was wondering why Nevada didn't pick up on that. Maybe Nevada just had too much else going on in his life to notice it. The Flying T2 Ranch brought on big responsibilities for its owner.

On Sunday morning after breakfast, Nevada took Ricki and TJ into Yuma to attend services at the church. Nevada was a nervous wreck. Nevada thought, *It's so darn long since I attended a church service. My bad luck would probably cause the church to burn down.* Their presence was immediately noticed by everyone when they walked in and sat down. The congregation couldn't help but stare at them and look around at each other. Nevada was feeling very uncomfortable, but he knew he was doing this for Ricki and TJ's benefit. It was something he needed to get used to as a new father. *Hell,* he thought, *I have been through much worse scrutiny than this before.*

After the services, the congregation assembled in the parish house for coffee and cake. Nevada was still nervous; however, it dissipated immediately when some ranchers approached him and started talking and asking questions about Nevada's raising rough stock for the rodeo circuit and the ranching business. He began to feel more relaxed because the conversation was to his liking. TJ ran over to Aunt Martha and Uncle John and gave them hugs. Then he went on to be with his school friends. Ricki socialized with the ladies, introducing herself as Nevada's wife. She had a sweet personality and was immediately liked by the ladies in town. The townsfolk felt, more sure than not, that this fine young lady with her spitfire personality was going to settle down the wild gunman, the Nevada Kid, and make him toe the line. In fact, they were all counting on it happening. So far, it looked like it was already beginning to work.

Before they left town, Nevada took Ricki over to meet Dr. Forrester. Dr. Forrester examined her and confirmed her pregnancy. The new baby would definitely be due in September. Nevada was worried about it because September was his busy season. There was usually a cattle drive to be done in the fall. Dr. Forrester promised Nevada that there was nothing to worry about. He inquired about Nevada's leg pain. Nevada assured him it was okay. Dr. Forrester did a good job on it nine years ago, and some of the strength was back with hardly any pain. He explained to Doc how his shoulder bothered him now.

"I took a bullet in my shoulder a year ago or so at the Broken Arrow Ranch. Somebody tried to dry-gulch me with a Winchester."

"Let me look at it, son," Doc checked it out. "I can see why it hurts. It got you in a tender spot. That shoulder will take a few years to heal." Nevada frowned at that statement. "I have some salve I can give you to ease the pain." He pulled the medication out of his cabinet. "Here you are. Put this on it before bedtime each night, and rub it in good. It will help the pain subside."

"Thanks, Doc."

They stopped by the general store for a few supplies. TJ got a peppermint stick and a new cowboy hat. Nevada didn't like the beat-up hat the kid was wearing and tried some new ones on him. When he found one he liked with a nice-shaped brim, he said to TJ, "What do you think?"

"Looks great, Pa! I like it. But is it too expensive?"

"Don't worry about the cost. I'm buying it for you. Ain't no kid of mine gonna look like a farm boy. We are ranchers, son."

Ricki just looked over at him and thought, *You still nursing that "farm boy, plow boy" notion? Get over it, Nevada.* She turned back, looking over some bolts of fabric for making infant clothes and blankets, and selected neutral colors that would work on a boy or a girl.

Nevada paid the clerk, and they left the store. When they got home, Nevada dropped Ricki and TJ off at the ranch house. Nevada took the buckboard back to the barn and unharnessed the team. Smokey approached him near the barn.

"How did it all go, Nevada?" inquired Smokey.

"Not bad for our first time at church. Everybody kept staring us down though. I had this uncomfortable feeling."

"Well, it ain't every Sunday they see a notorious gunman from the Younger Gang in church with his family. What did you expect from the townsfolk? They need a little getting used to you being around them and taking up their space."

"Well, I hope they get over it fast."

"You will have to prove yourself to them as an honest man for them to get over it, you know."

"Hell yeah, I know that. What's happening on the ranch today? Anything?" queried Nevada. "Where are all my ranch hands?"

"Today is the boys' day off. They all went into town this morning. They disappear on their day off faster than a double eagle in a brothel. But first thing tomorrow morning, I'm having them move the herd from the north range to the south range. Drought has caused the north range to be unusable, and I'm moving the herd to better grasslands. I really don't want that north range to become critically overgrazed. I'll make sure they move them without running any fat off the marketable steers."

"Smokey, cull out the bulls so we can keep them for breeding. One of those little rascals looked like a good bucker. He might make good rough stock for the rodeo. I need to take a closer look at some of them."

"Okay, Nevada. I planned on doing just that, boss. Hopefully, none of the men will be bitching with a bellyache when we get to the hard part of the work."

"Come up to the house and have supper with us tonight. I'll tell Ricki to put out another plate. Doc checked her today and said she is definitely pregnant and due in September."

"I hope that ain't gonna interfere with the trail drive to market. It could get rough for you trying to balance the work and the family."

"We'll worry about it when the time comes. I ain't gonna stress out over it now. TJ and I are going fishing this afternoon. I promised him."

"Sounds like fun. Wish I had the time to do some fishing. Remember when we used to fish together out on the trail?"

"How could I forget it? I thought you were going back to the horses for more bait, and instead you shoved me in the river. That was the second time you threw me in a damn river."

"Well, you needed a bath. I was getting tired of smelling your stink from my bedroll at night. You were as dirty as a flop-eared hound! Besides, it was funnier than hell watching you flopping around in the river in total shock!"

"You didn't have to hit me with the lye soap when you threw it in the river at me. I didn't smell that bad!"

"The hell you say. I was beginning to think you were plumb water shy! The whack with the lye soap was to give you a hint. Your damn shirt collar was so stiff and high from the dirt you had to mount a soapbox to spit. After that soaking, I was able to sleep again at night."

"Smokey, you may think you're being funny, but you are not."

"Well, Nevada, I think I'm funny. I have been keeping you amused for a hell of a lot of years."

"You have at that, pard. But I've been saving your sorry hide for just as many years, so we are even." They laughed together.

"Hey, Nevada, did you get a good look at TJ's horse?"

"No, why? Is something wrong?"

"He has the same markings as Rusty. Looks just like your pal Rusty. Any chance it could be Rusty's colt?" inquired Smokey.

"You don't say? Hell, let's go take a look at him." Nevada and Smokey went into the barn to look at Cinnamon. Nevada ran his hand down the rump and the withers, checking the horse all over. He looked at Smokey and whistled. "Same white socks on all fours. Same star on his forehead. Same birthmark on his rump. I got to ask TJ some questions about this horse." Nevada started tending to Cinnamon and brushing him down when TJ walked into the barn and up to Smokey and Nevada.

"Pa, what are you doing?" TJ inquired.

"Just tending to Cinnamon. I'll saddle him for you, and we can go fishing in a few minutes. How would you like that?"

"Yeah, Pa. I'd love it! I'll get the fishing poles out."

"Hey, TJ, before you do that, who sired this colt? Do you know? Was it a horse on Mr. O'Connors ranch?"

"Yeah, Pa. It was Ma's horse, Glitter, and a big old horse named Rusty. I remember how mad Uncle John was when Che Che Bean accidently put Rusty into the corral with Glitter. Glitter was separated into her own corral because she was in heat. Che Che Bean didn't know Glitter was in heat, and Rusty got her by accident when he put Rusty in the corral with her. Uncle John was so mad at Che Che Bean he fired him, and Che Che Bean went back to Mexico. But he wasn't mad because he said good-bye to me with a big laugh and a smile on his face. Che Che Bean said the foal was to be mine when it was born. I have been taking care of him ever since."

Nevada and Smokey looked at each other and couldn't stop laughing out loud. They were both thinking the same thing. *There's no way in hell Che Che Bean wouldn't know when a mare was in heat! John O'Connor knew it too, which is why Che Che Bean got fired.*

"Why are you laughing?" asked TJ.

"Because," said Smokey, "your pa owes Che Che Bean another big favor."

"Oh! Can we go fishing now?"

"Sure can," said Nevada. He finished saddling Cinnamon then saddled Tacco. He looped his guitar over his back, and Smokey handed him the homemade fishing poles.

"How come you are taking your guitar?" questioned Smokey.

"It's about time somebody teaches TJ how to play it," said Nevada with a wink.

"Oh! See y'all later. Good fishing," said Smokey.

When TJ and Nevada returned in time for supper, they had five nice-size brook trout with them. Smokey joined them for supper with graham-cracker cake for dessert. Smokey and Nevada were still giggling over how the succession of Rusty's lineage came about. Nevada was indebted to Che Che Bean forever. He would never have been able to preserve that bloodline from where he was, in prison, and there was no way John O'Connor had plans of doing it. Che Che Bean knew that full well. The bigger joke was that it was with Polly's horse, Glitter. So TJ and his horse, Cinnamon, had a lot in common as their bloodlines go, and Nevada won on both counts. He had his and Polly's son, and he had his and Polly's colt. As far as Nevada was concerned, he had achieved his goal, and his bad luck had now begun to change into good luck.

After supper, Smokey and Nevada went out on the porch to smoke and relax as they watched the sun setting on the Arizona horizon. Their private joke was the highlight of their night. Sandy stopped by to show Nevada the plans for the new addition on the house. Nevada liked the idea and approved of the plans. The foundation would be started as soon as possible. Nevada wanted it all done before the fall cattle drive north to the Denver stockyards. With the plans approved now, Sandy took them back to the tack shop and came back out with something of a surprise in his hands. When Ricki came out on the porch, Sandy presented her with a beautiful cradle he had made for the new baby. She loved it and was so excited. Sandy carried it inside for her and placed it by the fireplace.

"Now I can start making the bedding and quilt for it," she said. "I bought green fabric on Sunday, and I can't wait to get started." Ricki had just finished making dressing gowns for the new baby in green and yellow colors, staying away from pink and blue colors. If the new baby was a girl, she wanted to name it Carole Ann, and if it was a boy, Nevada wanted to name it Cimarron.

Sandy and Smokey said good night to Ricki and Nevada, then they headed back to the bunkhouse for a game of cards. They were anxious to get back to their quarters and relax with the other ranch hands.

Nevada sat alone for a long time on the porch just relaxing and enjoying the beautiful evening along with the sunset. His eyes surveyed all his rangeland and his cattle grazing way out there. He realized how far he came from the small farm he grew up on as a boy. That farm offered him nothing but aggravation and loneliness. Trouble seemed to follow him everywhere, and his pa was always whipping him for one reason or another. What a rotten childhood he had, although the farm taught him a lot about life, the raising of livestock, and growing things. It was hard work to reach the pinnacle of his goal to own a ranch, and the climb up the ladder was cumbersome and oftentimes painful. However, he got there, he accomplished his dream of owning a cattle ranch, and it was a good-size spread, even larger than he thought would be possible. God blessed him with a beautiful, intelligent, and caring wife and then blessed him again with the return of his son. Nevada felt that there wasn't another thing in his life he could ask for of God. Then he started to think about his adventure with Smokey in the mountains and the agony they went through to rescue their friend Cappie and get him back home. He supposed it was all worth the extended effort to get the job done and to get Cappie back home safely. Ricki came out on the porch and spoke to him.

"Nevada. I put on a fresh pot of coffee. Would you like a cup?"

"Yes, I would. Thanks, Ricki."

"Don't get up. Stay there. I'll fix it and bring it out on the porch to you."

Well, that is sweet of her, he thought.

She brought out the coffee and a piece of his favorite graham-cracker cake. "You are in deep concentration. What are you thinking about?"

"Our trip in the mountains and the ordeal we wound up going through."

"Oh, okay." She kissed him. "I'm getting ready for bed. It's getting late. Don't stay out too late. You are still a week behind in the ranch work."

"I'll be in soon. Where is TJ?"

"He is in his room doing homework from school. Don't forget to say *good night* to him when you come in."

"Okay, darlin'," replied Nevada.

Nevada picked up his guitar and started strumming some tunes, "The Wayward Wind" and "The Santa Fe Trail." The still evening air picked up his singing and carried it along like a gentle breeze moving across the rangeland, calming the livestock and encircling the bunkhouse where his range hands could hear him sing out in a calm, peaceful manner. His singing of ballads had a way of relaxing everything and everyone around him. A song dog wailed in the distance in answer to Nevada's melody. Tacco whinnied from the corral in answer to his master's voice. TJ momentarily stopped doing his homework to listen to his father's voice with a smile on his face. Ricki gently rubbed the movement of the growing child in her stomach while she rested in bed. The whole world seemed to stand still as it listened to Nevada's soft and low singing voice. He gently put down the guitar and started thinking again about his last trip into the mountains.

As Nevada sat on the front steps of his ranch house, he looked out at the purple majesty of the mountains surrounding his ranchland and had thoughts of the hunting trip, as well as the excitement and the dangers brought about by the adventure.

No wonder Cappie loved living in the mountains, thought Nevada. *There was never a dull moment, and there was something very magical about the mountains and the forest of ponderosa pines.* Nevada could hear Mother Nature whispering again throughout the distant mountain ridges. It was the kind of whispering magic one can only experience and never explain or put into meaningful words.

The magic of the animals silently living in the forest; the magic of their stalking, their mating, and their hunting for survival. The silent softness of the crayfish and the minnows swimming in the rushing sounds of the cool, clear brooks. The whispering wings of an eagle or a raven in flight coupled with the untamed spirit of the wild that takes one into many tomorrows. Mother Nature herself reached out farther than the stars to create this vast wilderness of whispering peace—a whispering peace that will go on forever until the end of time.

It was a whispering peace that can never be defined or matched in the big cities and small towns, created and built up by human hands, or for living in a vast, untamed country at the very end of this American frontier. Only God and Mother Nature at her finest can create the beauty of the mountain forest whispering in the silence of its living and growing things—living and growing in its own peace on earth.

Recipe for Graham-Cracker Cake
(Favorite of the Nevada Kid)
by Diane M. Cece

1/4 lb butter	1 c flour
1 c sugar	1 c graham cracker crumbs
2 eggs	2 tsp baking powder
1/2 c coconut	a pinch of salt
1 tsp vanilla	1 c milk

Cream butter and sugar together. Add one egg at a time and the coconut and vanilla and mix. Combine the dry ingredients. Add the milk to creamed butter/sugar mixture, and slowly add dry ingredients while mixing. Pour into two 8- or 9-inch pans. Batter is heavy; cake does not rise high. Bake in 375-degree oven for half hour.

Frosting:	1/4 c heavy cream	4 tsp melted butter
	confectioner's sugar	1 tsp vanilla

Mix confectioner's sugar with heavy cream to desired thickness. Add the butter and vanilla.

Edwards Brothers Malloy
Thorofare, NJ USA
September 29, 2014